D0655314

CRUSADE

BY
DONN BYRNE

LONDON
SAMPSON LOW, MARSTON & CO., LTD.

MADE AND PRINTED IN GREAT BRITAIN BY
PURNELL AND SONS, PAULTON (SOMERSET) AND LONDON

CRUSADE

CRUSADE

CHAPTER I

It seemed to the man on horseback, now that he was once more outside Jerusalem, now that from the Damascus gate he could see over the fortifications, over the huddle of houses, like the massed backs of turtles, the cupola of the Holy Sepulchre, and farther toward the left the miracle of cool delight that was the *Templum Domini*, the Temple of the Lord, and farther still, the blue mountains of Moab becoming purple in the sunset, that all his pain to be once more among his own people had gone. He blamed himself for wishing, as he knew he wished, he were still back in Damascus, a prisoner of the Saracen.

CRUSADE

Outside the Damascus gate Arabs were going to and fro. Sentinels in the green livery of the Count of Champagne were drowsing over their pikes. A mad knight, whom he remembered to have been a friend of Alenard, the norse crusader, galloped all but into him, and, raising his hands in the air, began to shout in barbaric Norman: "I see an eagle flying over a king's army, and in its claws are seven javelins. And it cries, Woe! Woe is Jerusalem!" He had a tangled red beard falling down to the pommel of his saddle, and unkempt red hair straggled about his winged norse helmet, and in his eyes, blue as a lake, was madness. The Arabs slippered away in respect from the man afflicted by God. But the green-jerkined sentinels laughed.

The man on horseback, for all his weakness as of a month-old child, forced his mare toward them, and called in fury: "How dare you insult a knight, you kept terrier? And where is your officer?"

The sentinels were small black men, with black Gaulish eyes. They were out of hand; impertinent.

"And whose kept man are you?" one sneered.

A gust of shaking anger came over him, with a throbbing in the head, and he remembered how he must appear to the sentinels. A man on a chestnut Arab horse, in silken Arab clothes, and the red boots of Syria on his feet, and on his face, he felt, the stamp of death. Yes, he must look like some renegade Christian, some of the many who had accepted Islam, and then been flung out of the tribes as a man lacking in honour, a man they didn't want. He noticed the Arab children eyeing him curiously, and a tonsured brother of Saint Francis—an Italian by his face—looking at him malignantly. An under officer hustled down from the tower, a spruce soldierly man.

"I am Sir Miles O'Neill," the man on horseback said, "attached to Sir Ulick de Lacy's command, and until four days ago a prisoner of the Saracens."

The man came to attention smartly enough, but Miles could see he had been drinking.

"Why don't you keep better discipline at your gate, man?" he asked.

"It is peace time, Sir Miles," the under officer answered, "and the men are lax." He dropped his voice. "It is so long since they have been paid, sir."

"Where is Sir Ulick's command?"

"I don't know, sir. If it was the Irish kerns, I'm afraid they're gone, sir. They were lost at the gaming tables, and went with their new owner into High Germany."

"And Sir Ulick?"

"Many of the knights have gone to Cyprus, sir."

O'Neill was silent. If this were so, he had come back penniless into a city where he had no friends. He would have to find lodging and food; an equipment, and a new commander.

"If you don't mind my saying so, sir," the under officer smiled, "you will find the Holy City changed. The peace will make a great difference, sir. Good for some, and bad for others. Good for me, sir. I've got a little property, sir, olive-trees and grapes near Bethlehem, and a little drove of camels."

"You are a Westminster man?"

"Southwark, sir."

"What English knight is in the city?"

"Let me think, sir. There's Sir Robert Paget, a Sussex man. Oh, a very nice knight, sir. And there's Sir Otho Trelawney, he's not English but a Cornishman. They call him, begging pardon, sir, Otho le Gras, a fat, swearing man."

"Where are Sir Otho's quarters?"

"Near the Temple, sir. I'd go with you, sir, but my relief doesn't come for an hour yet."

"I'll find it."

"Yes, sir. Thank you, sir." O'Neill rode off, thinking how the fellow would curse him for not having given him something. Dear God! How quickly the Holy Land rotted men!

As he rode down the crooked steep streets, the nauseous stench of Jerusalem almost stifled him, and he said to himself bitterly that he knew, beyond doubt, he was in a Christian city. A train of camels, whacked onward by Syrian Christians, bumped him against the walls, and his left arm, still in splints and sling under his coat, was scraped. A cold sweat broke out on his forehead, and a little groan came to his lips. A giant negro, clearing the street for a burly Templar, seized his mount's snaffle and forced it aside. He struck the Cairene convert across the face with the heavy whip in his right hand, cursing the officious black man so terribly, in such a chilled, low tone of voice that he shuffled away terrified. An English palmer, with mouth and eyes swollen and red from some hideous disease, implored him for alms with high whining patter, and when he, too, was cursed, retorted with such a flood of obscenity that it made the foul air fouler. O'Neill rode on. Chancing to glance downward he noticed that the chestnut's near fore hock was filling. That was the last straw.

And only four days ago he had left Damascus—clean and green and cool Damascus, where his captors were more friendly and more courteous than these brethren of his who bore the Cross on their shoulders as a sign of enduring fellowship. Enduring fellowship! he sneered. Were there ever such jealousies and such abominable treachery as obtained among the knights of the Cross? And yet he could not stay in Damascus.

Honour demanded he should return. But two months before, when it was decreed that Saracen and Christian should live in honourable peace, he had been happy. He had waited and waited to hear that his ransom had been paid. He had waited in vain. He had wondered if his commander, de Lacy, were dead. The old sheykh, whose prisoner he was, and the Arab physician, had remonstrated with him: "Sheykh O'Neill. Here are trees that bear apples and small rivers which sing songs. And many birds. And a mountain you can look at, Hermon with his white wise head. Let peace come into your heart, for only when there is peace in the heart can the body prosper. I would not extol myself," the old sheykh said, "but there are knights of Normandy who have been treated worse than you."

"I am but half Norman, Sheykh Haroun," O'Neill had said, "my father was of an impetuous, impatient race—the king of Ulster is my cousin. Chains break our wings. I can say so now that my ransom is on its way. It is not hardship, but that I have been a prisoner which irks me."

The old sheykh was silent for a full minute. They were sitting in the enclosed garden, fashioned after the pattern of the gardens of Cordoba in Spain, with plots of grass, and small orange trees and paths of golden gravel, and cool fountains. Sheykh Haroun drew letters in the path with his riding stick.

"Your ransom has been arranged, Sheykh O'Neill," he said quietly. The old physician looked at his chief in surprise.

O'Neill stood up and stretched his free arm. "Allaho Akbar!" he cried, in the words of the muazzin. "God is greatest! Who arranged my ransom, Sheykh Haroun?"

"A Certain One," said the sheykh.

"I asked," O'Neill grew cold, "what lord arranged my ransom?" He looked proudly at the Arab chief. The Arab looked at him just as steadily.

"The Lord of Daybreak, Sheykh O'Neill." O'Neill turned away with all the petulance of a sick man. He never felt so deserted, so small in all his life.

"Am I then so poor in friends and goods," he said bitterly, "that charity must be forced on me?"

"O boy," the old chief thundered, "I have said that He has ransomed you. And what compact this old man has made with the King of the Day of Fate is not your affair. Young sheykh, when will you learn that pride is a king in gold armour who hath a swine's snout? And take refuge from it as from Satan who was stoned?" He was silent a minute. "Also, I had thought that among the Arab you were not lacking in friends."

O'Neill's conscience turned restlessly in him.

"None could have been more kindly, more courteous than you have been, sir. I had thought it was just your chivalry. I had not dared to think it was more. . . . I am ashamed to have been so petulant."

"A sick man is but a helpless child," said the hakeem kindly. "His very weakness makes him angry."

"Do I not know that," said the old man, "who in my young time was wounded by King Richard's self?" He rose and came over to O'Neill, and his old hands, strong as oak, brown as old oak, took the horse's silver curb-chain that was like a bracelet on O'Neill's right arm—the only mark of his captivity. He broke it like a piece of rotted twine. O'Neill could believe now the stories of the old man's youth which had seemed like legends. Sheykh Haroun in combat with Richard at Assur had the king at his mercy, until the Lion-heart's bull-like rage and rush, and a little luck with an overarm swing with the mace—a farmer's blow!—had dropped the Bedouin chief with a broken shoulder-bone.

"You are no longer now a prisoner, but the guest of the Arab."

"A poor guest for a prince like you, Sheykh Haroun."

"What are riches but the length of God's tether? And are we not all guests? The guests of God!"

He noticed from the breaking of the chain a new feeling in the great household towards him. They were not less kind, but they were more formal. It was as if his status were changed. There was more respect— not that there had ever been lack of respect —but less sense of being heart to heart with all of them. He was not the poor dependent prisoner, but the equal of the sheykh. They spoke rarely of Islam before him any more, as though it would be bad manners to bring up religion before a Christian knight. The wound in his head had healed and the hurts in his side and chest from where his horse had rolled over him. But there was difficulty with the broken arm. That was progressing very well, all things considered, and he felt equal to the journey to Jerusalem.

"Sheykh Haroun," he told his host one evening, "in three days, or four days or five, I had better be going toward my commander's place."

There were present the sheykh and the physician, two of the younger chiefs, Mohammad and Abdallah, and Haroun's young daughter, Kothra, the "sister of Ali" as she was called, after Haroun's beloved eldest son, who was dead. She had changed more than anyone since he was free. She was so formal, so cold, and she had been so friendly. She was spoiled by everyone, and yet unspoiled, the sister of Ali. She sat there, cross-legged, dressed like a young sheykh of the desert, her head-dress drawn across the lower part of her lean, pearl-white face. Her hands white, thin, nervous, unstained by henna, played with a light bamboo riding stick. . . . The old sheykh passed three more beads of his beautiful amber rosary through his fingers.

"Will you not stay with us, Sheykh Mael-morra?" he asked. "There is so little between you and us. I ask pardon for this, but the Arab, knowing it is good, wishes to share Islam."

"I cannot, Sheykh Haroun," O'Neill said. "I am sorry. It would not be to my honour. The Arab understand that."

The sister of Ali said nothing. She drew graceful Arab letters in the sanded space at her feet. The young chieftains, Mohammad and Abdallah, nodded gravely.

"Surely the Arab understand that," Abdallah murmured. "To live without honour is to walk bent in two."

"But why do you want to go so soon?" the sister of Ali asked. There was something keen and musical about her voice, like a high clear note on the viol, or the ring of a gold bezant on marble. "As yet you are not a healed man."

"Because I hunger for news of my friends, and the taste of Frankish speech, sister of Ali, and for the wail of the Irish pipe as the gallow-glasses mourn for their distant land. And my dogs are pining for me, and they go around, I know, questioning everyone with their brown eyes, and they cannot understand. Though I know what science the hakeem has," he looked gratefully at the physician, "he understands that among my own folk my arm will heal."

"Sheykh O'Neill speaks truth," said the hakeem. "Do I not remember, when a student in Seville, that I used to walk by the green river, and weep a little for deserted Arabia, the wastes of Keybar, and the camel colts I was born among! All the Bedouin understand."

"You will need some gold pieces," said the old sheykh. "You will not refuse them from the Arab, your friends."

O'Neill flushed. He was not sure he wouldn't need them, but he was not going to be beholden any more. He was beholden for his life, for his liberty, to the chivalry of the Arab, and by the Very Cross of God! though he starved, he would take no more.

"I shall be well provided, Sheykh Haroun, once I cross the Jordan. Excuse me for refusing, but I shall be well when there. There is only one thing, if I might borrow a horse——"

"You cannot borrow," said the sister of Ali, "I give you mine."

"I cannot accept it, sister of Ali."

"Then walk!" Her voice had the clear ring of a sword.

There was a pause of embarrassment. The young chiefs looked at each other with a surprise in their eyes. The hakeem was bothered. The old sheykh sat up, rigid with anger.

"O sister of Ali," he thundered, "have you no shame in your father's house? Are these Arab manners, an Arab heart? Sheykh O'Neill, pardon this mad Bedouin girl. Whatever horse you wish you will take and send it back when you will."

From behind the sister of Ali's head-dress, clear over the splash of the fountain and the song of an early nightingale, O'Neill caught a muffled sob.

"If I may, Sheykh Haroun, I shall accept the horse of the sister of Ali."

The old hakeem laid his hand on O'Neill's shoulder. Mohammad turned to Abdallah. "Ho! by God! this is courtesy!" he said. The old man bent his eyes on his daughter. "Hearest thou, girl, what honour our guest does thee?"

"I ask his pardon," she said nervously, "and yours, father of Ali."

"And God's!" insisted the old man.

"The Compassionate, the Compassionating," the sister of Ali murmured.

Through the soft Damascene dusk, the dusk of chiming river and nightingales and the scent of pear and almond blossom, came the call of the muazzin from the minaret of the Bride; "Allaho Akbar." Something in the faint throbbing tones had the call of distant, imperious drums. "God is greatest! God is greatest!" The Bedouin chieftains rose.

"We shall leave you to rest yourself, Sheykh O'Neill." O'Neill knew they were off to evening prayer. "I assert there is no God but God! I assert that Mohammad is the Messenger of God!" went the blind watchman. O'Neill touched forehead and heart in response to their farewell. Only the sister of Ali lingered.

"I am very sorry, O'Neill, for behaving like a child." O'Neill saw tears around the fringes of her eyes.

"It is not that I didn't wish to accept a gift from you, sister of Ali, but I have had so much, and I am ashamed."

"From us you have had no more than a rose from a garden whereby the thousand roses grow. I understand, O'Neill." She was bothered under the call of the importunate, imperious muazzin. "I am pardoned, O'Neill?"

"You embarrass me, sister of Ali," he said uncomfortably.

"Then I am pardoned," she smiled with her eyes, and putting fingers to forehead, disappeared after her father and cousins. . . .

Though only four days ago since he had left, it seemed an age, so different was the atmosphere of Jerusalem from that grave courtesy and kindly wisdom. Once he had crossed the Jordan from the Saracen country, he had not found the hospitality and help he had boasted of to Sheykh Haroun. In the Hospitallers' station at Nazareth, he had been herded with cripples and beggars and flung a crust of bread, a handful of olives, and given tepid water in a jug with the handle broken. There was no use in insisting he was a knight. Of poor knights the roads were full. On the road to Tiberias he had had a bit of luck. He had overtaken a fat, greasy-bearded merchant on a mule, who spoke the Mediterranean Frankish dialect. He was a Hungarian, he said, and had come to visit the Holy Places. "And what was your Highness?" he asked, looking suspiciously at O'Neill's Arab silks. "An English, or rather an Irish knight, until yesterday a prisoner of the Saracen."

"Then you have an oath to protect pilgrims, yes?"

"Yes," O'Neill said carelessly.

The man breathed a sigh of relief and settled down on his mule. He was fat as a fat woman. O'Neill noticed that his hands were black with grime, except for broad lines on the fingers of comparative whiteness. The man had been wearing rings and had taken them off and concealed them. He noticed egg on the Hungarian's whiskers, and his own hunger of a convalescent began to clamour. He wished he could pull his waistband tighter. . . . So his Highness had been a prisoner of the Saracens! In chains! No! Free! Well it was good to be a knight! So his Highness was well-treated! The Hungarian edged closer. Did his Highness see the Arab women? The merchant's tongue went over his lips. Of course he didn't know himself, but he had heard travellers' tales. They were free and lively, the women of the Saracen, and most vicious. They did this. They did that. Did his Highness have any adventures in his captivity? He leered.

"I don't know if you understand me, merchant, but your conversation seems to me of a singular filthiness."

Oh! His Highness was a good knight, a holy knight! The merchant was so relieved. One heard such stories of the licence in Palestine. Such things were said of the Knights Templars——

"Let me give you one word of advice," warned O'Neill, "that may save you your goods, and maybe your life. Curse God if you wish in the street of el-Kuds—of Jerusalem, I mean—but say no word against the Templars."

So! Oh! he was glad to hear that, the merchant said. Oh! he would not make a mistake like that for the jewels of the Emperor! Was his Highness a Knight Templar?

"No," O'Neill said shortly.

Yes, a merchant couldn't be too careful, the Hungarian said. He must be friends with everybody. Of course it was a secret, but he didn't mind telling his Highness. Besides saving his soul in the Holy Land, there was an opportunity of making some profit. Did his Highness know that the wines of Palestine were soft and sweet like honey? No! Well they were, and did his Highness know the price? No! One tenth of what Tokay cost. He had in mind to buy and ship in Joppa wine for Pola. And there put it in bottles and sell it as Tokay in Venice. Venetians accustomed to their harsh Italian wine could not tell the difference.

Oh, not nobles, not people like his Highness, but burghers, traders, such as Venice was full of. Oh! his Highness did not know how well a merchant could get on. Figure! Only this morning he had sold his horse to a Hospitaller at a great profit, and bought this mule for the smallest possible trifle, because its back was skinned.

"Get off!" O'Neill reined up.

"But—"

"Get off!"

The man slid off clumsily, speaking something in his hissing tongue.

"Unbuckle the girths and remove the saddle!"

He looked at the mule's back and all but vomited.

"You walk the rest of your way," he said. "Give me that bridle."

"But you have sworn to protect pilgrims," the man squealed.

"Pilgrims, yes," O'Neill spoke furiously, "but not every damned scavenger who comes to profit in the land fertilized by Crusaders' blood. Do you think it was for a louse paddock like you that Tancred and de Bouillon fought? Oh! shout if you like,

These barren rocks are laughing at you
And now five pieces of gold."

"For what?" The man stopped shouting
and looked at him.

"For my comfort and sustenance."

"I have none."

O'Neill took his right foot out of his stirrup
and caught the mule's bridle on it. He
reached into his waistband and drew the
beautiful Damascene blade, greater than dagger and less than sword, which was Abdallah's
parting gift. "You will save me a lot of
trouble by not arguing."

The man fumbled in his greasy breast.
"God will strike you!" he threatened.

"Not at all," O'Neill smiled. "God will
uphold me utterly." He put the blade between his teeth while he took the money.
"And now, the nearest station of soldiers
is fifteen miles from here. You had better
get there before nightfall. There are mad
lepers in the hills." And picking up his
reins he trotted off.

It didn't bother his conscience much. He
had done an hundred times more criminal
things in the name of the Cross, raids against
Bedouin tribes for horses and sheep, holding

the Arab prisoners to ransom. It was a rough world. However, he had enough now to last him and his horse in dignity to Jerusalem. Five miles onward he sent the mule bucketing up the hills with a flick of his whip.

He felt so weak now after his four days' ride that he was ashamed of himself. A trembling as of fever was in his knees and heels. And now, as he guided his mount down the narrow streets, he came under the shadow of the Temple, and the old unreasonable fear came into his heart. It was so quiet, so big, so—deadly. Its power had overcome the mortal life of the Lord Jesus. Its riches had tempted Roman and Babylonian. The Romans and Babylonians were lighter now than desert dust. But the vast courses of masonry laid by Solomon, and King Hiram, and Hiram out of Tyre, remained as foundations and would remain, it seemed, for ever. What toll of lives it had exacted! And what loyalty was given to it. Even now as he passed the entrance, the mailed and mounted sentries had faces out of which all human kindliness had gone. They were hard as the granite of the Rock. They were aloof, mysterious as the Rock. In the Lord's time it was death to speak against the Temple. It was death to-day.

He rode past it down the narrow *sooq* to the old Saracen house whither he had been directed. A vast Egyptian eunuch, bloated like a frog, sat in a niche by the nail-studded door.

"Is this Sir Otho Trelawney's house?"

"Yes," the door-man said, and "sir" he added as O'Neill kept his grey eyes trained on the hideous obese face.

"I wish to see Sir Otho. Open your door!"

"But I cannot open, sir, until I know your business—"

"The business of the Holy Cross. Open!"

The vast bulk padded in its heelless slippers, unloosening bolt and catch. He wheezed like some monstrous water animal. O'Neill rode into the courtyard. The place was dim and cobbled. It seemed darker than the dark streets. In a corner where a meagre shaft of sunlight came, a man as young as himself, in black hose and a silk coat, was strumming at a Provençal guitar . . .

. . . *Le Rommant de la Rose,*
Ou l'art d'amors est toute enclose.

"The Romance called the Rose," he sang,
"whose verse all love's sweet stratagem enclose."

He had a blunt, half-Saxon face, and hair
like flax. His hands, O'Neill saw, were never
made for any musical instrument, nor his
voice for any Norman song. A page-boy
came toward O'Neill's stirrup.

' I wish to see your master, boy. I am an
Irish knight, Miles O'Neill of Lucan." While
the boy hurried off, the man in the corner
kept on with his song:

"*Maintes gens dient que en songes*
"*N'a ses fables et mensonges;*

"So many say that in dreams' ecstasies,
the clear-cut scenes are but the Foul One's
lies,"

"*Mais j'en . .   *"

' But I .   "

Both voice and music went off at grotesque
angles The player grinned and threw the
instrument down. He strolled over toward
O'Neill.

'Don t seem to get the swing of it." He
smiled ruefully "Never could handle these

French songs." He was short and thick-set with a rough, kindly face. "You're Irish, aren't you?"

"I am."

"Kent man myself. From the Weald, as we call it. Josselyn my name is. Did I hear you say you were called Miles O'Neill?"

"You did."

"Got some cousins in Dublin myself." He grew embarrassed.

"I say," he looked at O'Neill, "wasn't— wasn't Miles O'Neill killed in a sort of raid against Big Jenico Fitzpaul? Good while ago. About twenty years, or more."

"He was. I am the younger Miles O'Neill."

"I'm sorry." Josselyn blushed. "But you know what times are. You'd have been worried yourself, if you understand. I say won't you get down? Take it easy? I don't know if you noticed, but your horse has gone lame, I think."

O'Neill felt a faintness wash over him, like a slow curling wave. He put his hand to his forehead and was surprised to find the palm wet when he took it away.

"You fool!" he said. "You damned fool! Can't you see that if I get off this horse I shall fall?"

The Kentish man sprang forward to catch him in case he should drop. "Ho, Giles, Fulke, Henry." His voice went like thunder through the courtyard. "Cross of God! Where are you all? Fall in and help me with this hurt gentleman. No, not that way," he directed O'Neill. "Throw your right leg over the horse's neck and slide down. I'll catch. There! That's it. I've got you! Good!"

CHAPTER II

THOUGH he had very solemnly cursed Ireland
from the deck of the Flemish merchant's
boat as Two-Rock and Three-Rock Mountains became small purple islands and then
faint clouds in the west, yet in the three years
he had been in the Holy Land he felt his
mind and heart going back there. The soft
Erse of nurse and huntsman came to him
more easily than the Norman tongue. He
remembered the terrific fight outside Bethlehem two years before, when all seemed lost.
The Saxon bowmen were falling back before
the crash of Ameer Yussuf's light cavalry,
hampering de Lacy's Irish clansmen. De
Lacy himself could do nothing. "*Poussez-
en-avant!*" the big man was thundering.
Some old strain in O'Neill gave out the
Ulster battle-cry. "*Lauv derg!*" he called
the cry of the O'Neills. "Red hand! Red

Hand!" And the Irish had caught the trumpet of their native speech. Suddenly, in a grey-brown froth, they pressed forward like a pack of their own wolf-dogs, baying like wolf-dogs. "*Lauv derg!*" they sobbed. "Red Hand! Red Hand!" The picked Arab cavalry could not withstand these battle-mad kerns. He would have liked his silent, fastidious, Norman mother to have heard him then!

Not anything of the formal castle at Lucan came back to him, but of the country. Soft Liffey rolling toward the sea, the leap of a trout, the swirl of salmon, the banks edged with rushes, the lazy cawing of rooks in the high trees, the cattle of mottled brown and gold. The mountains of Wicklow, purple as a purple cloak. The little Danish city of Dublin, so neat, so precise. One would liken it to a little city of High Germany— small, compact houses, with beds of tulips, and little greens, where the Danes before their dispersement used to sit and drink ale, and the King of Dublin would come out, like any burgess, and sit and drink with them. A quiet town of high gabled houses and florid merchantmen, and now the Normans, with their cold efficiency were building castles and turning the dreaming city into a battlemented stronghold, with their blue-eyed, cold-mannered masons from Chartres and Rouen. Well, the Normans were better for the city, O'Neill thought, than his father's people. When they took Dublin from the Danes they ruined it. Dirt was everywhere. They cut down the growing trees for firewood, and the formal greens and beds of tulips were trampled into a farm midden. The quaint alleys were the peep-holes of cut-purse and cut-throat. Of course it was inevitable that the Normans should have come in, if civilization were to remain in the green land. But need they have been so cold, so superior, so damned ruthless? And their politics, their alliances! In their great Nordic frames was there any heart?

Of the great houses of Lucan, he had none but memories which chilled him. There lived his mother, with her spare body, tall and bare and uninviting as the high poplars that lined the roads of Normandy. She had hands white and fragile as the hands of a skeleton, and between them was always a book of hours. Her face was pointed like

a fox's mask. Her chin was sharp. Her
mouth was too small, too red. Her green
eyes were rimmed with red. When she
would be an old woman, she would resemble
the popular concept of a witch. His uncle
Jenico, whom his father had killed, and
whose followers had killed his father, had
been described to him as a great, lumbering
man, with a cruel twist to his mouth, and a
harsh laughter, cold and grating like the
east wind. His other uncles he hated, the
Abbot of Kells, more warrior than monk,
who boasted that if he were lax in keeping
the gates of Heaven, the Irish or the Fitzgeralds who might think the gates of Kells
were easy had only to come and try; his
uncle Foulke, the hunchback with the absurdly
beautiful face—absurd in its calm beauty
above the horrible body. The face of Foulke
was not an index to his mind, but his
hands were. They were crooked, predatory,
covered terribly with light brown hair. In
that trait you could see the secretive, treacherous, the subtle spider. His life was dedicated
to getting the better of the Fitzgeralds, to
wresting the control of Leinster from them into
the hands of the Fitzpauls. In his heart

he saw himself, Miles knew, as that strange insect of building tradition, the Sharmah, drilling through the foundations of the edifice of good faith and kindliness the Fitzgeralds had built in Ireland. But the Fitzpauls would never get the better of the Geraldines, Miles knew. There was some strange bond of loyalty between the Fitzgeralds and the Irish. Indeed, the Geraldines were becoming, said the other Norman families, more Irish than the Irish themselves.

Himself, Miles knew now, so far was he from home, and so easy was it for him to see at this distance in true perspective what at home was concealed from him by the tissue of half-lies his relatives had spun, was the victim of a political marriage. His father had been a worse victim than he, but his father was dead now, and so far as his father's life went the Lord of Justice would exact a terrible accounting from the Fitzpauls.

His father had been a younger son of the main family of O'Neill, kings of Ulster, the warlike northern clan who were co-lords with the O'Donnells, and chieftains of the Gallaghers and of Mac Sorley of the Battle-

Axes. Of all the northern families they were the only one who accepted the European ranking of knight and esquire. Many of them had fought against the Saracen in Spain, sailing out of Donegal to Lisbon and Cadiz, and taking service with the king of Spain. They had little to do with England, their friendship being with the Scottish king. They were a difficult family, great fighters, great dreamers—Niall of the Nine Hostages had visioned a Celtic Empire great as that of Rome, with Ireland, Scotland, Cornwall and Wales, and Brittany of France joined in an enduring brotherhood, but that needed politicians, and the O'Neills were not politicians, they were fighters. They were proud and self-sufficient. They never aimed at the High Kingship of Ireland, but except at their invitation no High King could pass through the gap of the North at Newry, or over the Erne. Such Norman knights as had fought their way through had been either forced to recognise the suzerainty of O'Neill or were driven back into the Pale. His father had had two estates, one on the windy slopes of Tanderagee in Down, now held by an uncle, and the other at Lucan.

a pleasant tumbled-down place which had come into the family through a marriage with the Wicklow clan of O'Moore. His father, Maelmorra Auling, Miles the Magnificent, as the native Irish had called him, had been a good-humoured, various man. Great-framed, charitable, ready to match a falcon or a deer- or wolf-hound with anybody for a big stake, or race a Welsh pony up the slopes of Three-Rock against any Norman baron. The Abbot of Kells had proposed his sister to the elder Miles in marriage, pointing out the advantages of an union with the Fitzpauls. The abbot had in his mind the advantage of the union of the Fitzpauls with the chiefs of Ulster. A nephew of the King of Ulster! But the abbot, for all his cunning, did not understand Ae Doragha, Dark or blind Hugh O'Neill, who spent most of his time in the Abbey of Donegal, praying like the humblest hermit, and who considered his sons' and nephews' lives of hunting and hawking with the ignorance of the blind and the aversion of the fanatic.

Young Miles could see his father, in his laughing way, consenting. And then Pernella

Fitzpaul came into Lucan, and with her coming, sport and magnificence went. He understood the Norman way. This was bad taste; that was not done. The nobles of Charlemagne and the men of Charles Martel had a code that investigated all the corners of honour. A knight did not wear, as his father wore, great armlets of gold captured from the store of old Danes. He did not wear red cloaks and greaves of gold. A gentleman did not argue with his huntsman as with an equal. A gentleman did not let an old servant berate him for giving too much for a horse. A gentleman did not sit on a wall to listen to a goatherd's fiddling. All a gentleman did, evidently, was to give orders. It must have been terribly irksome for his father to have to look over his shoulder to see if wife or relative-in-law were looking before he bestowed a gold Danish-minted coin on a huntsman who had shown him a good wolf or deer, or a minstrel who had played for him a beloved air. For the Normans were economical.

"A gentleman doesn't waste his money."

"What does a gentleman do with it, then?"

"A gentleman buys power."

'Friends are power. I've got all the power I want."

"Friends change," said the subtle Normans. "Better solid masonry and tried men-at-arms."

"*Jarar mochree Kriestha!* Christ, brother of my heart!"

"Hush! A gentleman doesn't curse that way. He says: *Foy de gentilhomme!* or *Dieu me garde!*"

"It seems to me," young Miles had heard that the elder Miles had complained, "that in giving up Irish chieftainship for Norman gentility, I have quit the ways of a free man for the manners of a mercer's bastard."

They had changed everything, these Normans. Even the gentle Irish monk of the mystic traditions of Brigit and Columcille, barefoot, white-robed, ringing his little bell against demons and the excommunicate, praying to God amid the heather and under the giant Irish oaks, so joyful that Christ had risen, was giving way to the polished Norman clerk, part warrior, all politician, whose song was the *Dies iræ*. At Lucan, the elder Miles found himself growing lonelier and lonelier. The old companions who would hunt all day with him, and drink all night, drinking rhenish wine out of three-handled silver flagons, while the fire blazed on the courtyard, who used to gamble for a gold piece a point with dice of polished elk-bone, were all gone now. They gave this reason and that reason, but the real cause was the grave, cold Norman woman with whom under a roof it was impossible to be merry. Before he married, many a night the woods of Lucan had rung to old Irish songs of a more lawless age: " *A Togail nan Bo;*" "The Lifting of the Cattle," while they drank the door-draught, *deoch an dorais*, before cantering home under the silver Irish moon. Ah, old companions! Where were you now?

Little by little, even the Irish servants were sent away, and Norman pages and valets began to take their places, men who would do women's work, servants who were very respectful, but who, the Irish knight felt, despised the men of the country. He had overheard one refer to the Irish as the "mere Irish," and had given him a dressing with the deerskin hound-whip. But his wife had been coldly furious

CRUSADE

When Jenico and Foulke had come over from Caen, Jenico ostensibly to look for a small estate, and Foulke to keep his sister company for a while, Big Miles had thought the old times would come back, that it would be once more a man's house, where again the shaggy wolf-dogs could lie before the fire in the rushes. But the hunchback Foulke was more finicky than any woman. Beneath Jenico's great frame he was coldly racial. When Jenico spoke his blue eyes were always watching you to see what effect his words had. You were always in mental battle with Jenico. Always measuring his words, was Jenico, as the Norman guest houses, O'Neill thought contemptuously, measured their thin wine. " Damn it!" thought the Irish chief, "did a man as big as Jenico have to be so careful! Couldn't he out with a thing: 'That's what I mean, and if you don't like it, God's Blood! what do you intend to do?' That's how a man felt." No, Miles the Magnificent could not stomach Jenico. And as to the hunchback, Foulke, all O'Neill's mountain straight-forwardness revolted against his concealed tortuous mind.

And now neither Jenico nor Foulke nor

the Abbot of Kells, no, nor his wife, Pernella, would give him an instant's peace
but that he must have Lucan fortified,
according to the latest rules of the art. The
hunchback had a genius for fortification, it
seemed, and had a plan for moating Lucan,
drawing the water from Liffey of the Herons.
Also, dressed stone was cheap. It could be
taken from old Danish houses and towed up
the river.

" But what need for fortifications? " O'Neill
asked. " Am I not friends with everyone—
with nearly everyone? "

O'Neill, they suggested quietly, did not
understand high policy. Of course everyone could see that England and Scotland
were orienting toward war. What rewards
O'Neill could ask from the English king,
once the war over!

"But we would stand with the Scot!"

Jenico's eyes closed to inimical slits.
Foulke hissed like a snake. His wife's
mouth grew tight and prim. But the
Abbot of Kells gave his laugh like faint
thunder:

"Then, *Dieu me damne!* " he swore, "what
a stronghold for the King of Scots!"

38

O'Neill had fingered the long amber necklace he wore that had belonged to great Thorkil the Dane.

"There would be no Irish chieftain with as strong or as fine a fortress as yours, brother," insinuated Foulke.

"Yes, yes," wavered O'Neill, and then: "But I can't afford this thing."

"Ho, then, O'Neill, what are you wedded to?" The Abbot was hurt. " A dowerless bride? What family have you allied with? A sept of straw? What are the Fitzpaul riches for, but to help our friends? You are more than our friend. You are our brother."

In the end he agreed, and his northern estate calling his attention, he was glad to get away. Pernella was difficult also. Of course that was easily explained. She was with child. Well, she was with her brothers. Up north, he was happy, coursing on the hills of Down, fishing for salmon in lough Neagh, hunting the wild boar and the wolf in the woods about the Bann. The Abbot of Kells sent letters for him asking him to keep away. "Frankly, this building you would not enjoy. We Norman pismires like it, but the Irish hawk for the hills." O'Neill was glad to stay away. The old life in Lucan was duplicated here, except for racing and rhenish wine. He preferred the crisp wine of the Rhine vineyards to the sweetness of the wine of Spain and Portugal that came around by sea to Carrickfergus. But the coursing of hares and the hunting of boars were better here. Then came news of his son's birth. "Pernella was delivered of a boy on Saint Enda's day," wrote the Abbot. "They wished to call him after Jenico, but I baptized him Miles. She is gone to rest a little at Skerries. There is no haste home, brother. I have your affairs at heart. Man, are we not like Boaz and Jachin, we two, apart, but a mysterious unit! Your brother on earth and *in Christo*, Hugue de Kells." Something told O'Neill he should start at once for Lucan.

A great rage, like the fabled rage of the Norseman, came over him when he saw his house. He would hardly have known it. Here and there masons were working like ants, while oxen dragged great blocks of stone on slips over the trampled grass. A great dingy drain was about the house, where small roses had grown, and worst of all, for

three furlongs' distance from the walls
every tree was down—old friendly trees
where the white deer had roved, and which
were the resting place of the wise rooks. Oh!
Champion of Heaven! This was too much.
For all his masculinity O'Neill could have
cried. Never, never did he dream such a
thing could have been done. Everywhere
were stolid Norman archers. He flung his
way into the hall where Foulke was at his
tracing board, with Jenico bent over him.
He was about to rush at Jenico when his
fighter's instinct told him that the house was
alive with daggers.

"What have you done to my house, Fitzpaul?" he asked, shaking with anger.

"We have modernized it, as your wish
was," said Jenico, quietly, too quietly.

"You have torn up flowerbeds tended by
generations of O'Moore women, and you have
cut down ancient kindly trees. And you
have made a barracks of a friendly dwelling-
place. That was not my wish. Whose are
these bowmen?"

"Mine, if you will ask," said Jenico.

"Clear them out, and out with you and
your brother!"

"Lightly, lightly, O'Neill," the big Norman laughed. "You would have us spend money, good Norman money, and brains, keen, Norman brains, on your Irish barn, and then tell us: 'get out.' Ah, it is not as easy as that! Is this the Irish game? Teeth of God!" he laughed, "what fools you must take us for!"

"Where are my wife and child?" O'Neill asked.

"The Lady Pernella and her son are with the Fitzpauls of Skerries," Foulke answered in his silky voice.

"And Hugue of Kells?"

"The Abbot of Kells is on a visit to Cashel."

"Ha! The fox is gone to earth."

"Oh, brother!" Foulke raised his hands in protest.

"Christ!" but O'Neill remembered in time the man's crippledom. He turned to Jenico. "You at least speak a man's tongue. Pernella and her child are in the hands of the Fitzpauls. Your brother avoids me. You and your archers are holding Lucan. I take it the next move is mine."

"If you wish to move," mused Jenico. "Why move?"

O'Neill smiled grimly. " Because you walked into England, you think you can over the Celtic lands. By God! Fitzpaul, don't you know you have to do with Red Hand?"

"Red Hand will find its palm full, I think, in the coming strife with the MacDonnells, Lords of the Isles, and with Yellow Mac Sorley."

"Now, how the hell does he know that?" O'Neill pondered.

"And I can't see Dark Hugh," went on Jenico, "bothering about the marriage disagreement of a nephew he has never particularly liked."

"I was never a man of tricks," Big Miles answered. "If you won't get out, I must put you out."

"You can always try," said Jenico dryly.

Riding northward, Miles tried to enlist help at Dundalk and Newry, but the response was small. He gathered a few friends in Oriel, and sending up to Tanderagee with the message: "Follow me up to Dublin!" he rode for Lucan. He rode as an Irish chieftain, armed only with dagger, battle-axe, and targe. And leaving his friends in the wood, he walked forward toward the battlements of Lucan

"Come out, Jenico," he roared, "come out and be killed."

Jenico was no coward. He came out alone. He wore light chain mail and helmet, and carried his shield and long Norman sword.

"I want no speeches," O'Neill warned. "I'm going for you."

For a big, clumsy-looking man, Jenico was quick as a greyhound. The long sword went out with every ounce of weight behind it. It glittered in O'Neill's eyes as he slipped sidewise, turning on his left foot. Jenico jumped back, and came again, not giving the Ulsterman a chance to swing with the battle-axe. The sword-blade was cold and blue, but not colder or bluer than Jenico's eyes. O'Neill could see that Jenico was for killing him. That made things simpler.

The point of the sword, with the afternoon sunlight on it made a flickering light in the air, like a marshlight seen when the moon is dark. The only sound was the shuffle of Jenico's feet in the grass, and his heavy breathing in his nostrils. O'Neill was crouching, circling with the light movements of a cat.

O'Neill stood up suddenly, frowning, as if puzzled. His bronze-studded shield was hip

high, and his axe by his knee. Jenico thought
he saw his chance. He went for O'Neill's
throat, a beautiful lightning lunge. Big Miles
dropped and let the sword go over his
shoulder. And then swinging upward and
inward, the battle-axe caught Jenico in the
cleft of the chin, dividing the fore front of his
head like a shared apple. The axe followed
its arc over O'Neill's left shoulder.

As O'Neill stepped back and looked at the
fallen Norman, an arrow from the battlements
knocked him dead and broken like a bird
struck with the shot of a sling.

The Irish kerns broke from the woods like
unleashed wolf-dogs. Calmly the Norman
archers began picking them off as in a quiet
shooting contest. Leaving three-fourths of
their number like broken dolls on the grass,
the score odd of living retreated. They saved
Big Miles' body, hoping to bring it to Ulster.
But the pursuit was too hot for them and they
buried Big Miles by the way. They buried
him at Broo of the Boyne, in the old Irish
and very pagan manner of which the Church
disapproved, that is: standing upright in his
grave with his axe in his hand, and his face
toward his enemies. And, swearing to the

dead man that, by God! they would be back again, they fled for Slievegullion, stealing horses that they foundered by the way. Every hand in the Pale was against them, so that of the hundred men who set forth, with O'Neill, only two returned to relate the harrying. The young O'Neill chiefs posted to Donegal Abbey to get the king's permission to wage war. But the blind king was against war, except with the MacDonnells and Mac Sorley Boy. He assured the young men that, after prayer, he would do what was best in the matter. The king's blindness saved him from the sight of anger and shame in the young warriors' faces, but even had he seen them, it would have wrought no change in his harsh, gnarled mind. He did, as he promised, what seemed best to him. He had masses said for Big Miles' soul.

CHAPTER III

In quiet Lucan the younger Miles grew up a patient, self-contained boy. He would never be as big as his father, but about his face was an Irishry that bothered the Fitzpauls, bothered Foulke, the spider, bothered the flaxen-haired Abbot of Kells. His curly black hair and grey eyes had nothing Norman in them, but he had Norman gravity, Norman patience. He bothered some of his tutors. The old captain of *hobilers* who taught him horsemanship, and the lean Italian-Englishman at Dublin, who was master of fence, found him an exacting pupil. The lay-brother of Kells who taught him literature, found him interested, but not over keen. He learned the beauties of Virgil, Augustus' poet, and of Theocritus, who was the pride of Ptolemy. He got to know something of the pure and sinewy Horace; the clear-phrased Juvenal; the witty

Martial; Seneca, echo of the Grecians; Statius, whom his teacher considered a better poet than Horace: Plautus, whom Varro called the mouth of Muses, and that English Archbishop, Joseph of Exeter, whose Latin the Germans thought was of Cornelius Nepos. From the lay-brother he also learned history, cosmography, and the knowledge of blazonry. But all that pertained to warfare was curiously interesting to him, and, strangely enough the best tutor he could have ever found was the cripple Foulke. None had studied the inwards of the matter more. From him young Miles learned of the campaigns of Alexander, and of Scipio Africanus: and the use of rams, testudos and all the engines of siege. Foulke made him even drill the pikemen like the commonest sergeant. The courtyard resounded with the clatter of shafts. Young Miles, under the eye of the seated cripple, gave the orders: "Advance pikes!"; "Shoulder!"; "Order!"; "Check!"; "Port!"; "Comport!"; "Order your pikes!" It was strange that the man of least use in war like this crippled one should know most of it.

About the whole of Lucan there was, it seemed to the boy, the sense of decay. For all the cleared spaces about the house, it seemed that the house was dark. Carp and trout in the moat never thrived, and for all the gardener's care, flowers would not grow freely. And yet, in the old days, so the Irish said, no place was more kindly to bird and flower. All the Fitzpaul gold could not breed gold of primroses. All the Fitzpaul silver could not lure the silver note of birds. Age had not sculptured into lines of dignity Uncle Hugue's face. The bluff hilarity of the Abbot of Kells deceived no man now. His wide, thin mouth and shabby eyes were danger signals even to the most gullible. Uncle Foulke's white features grew more beautiful, but with the dark beauty of evil. Miles' mother moved through the house like a thin ghost. Now, in Palestine, Miles knew she had been privy to his father's death, and that the weight of it was too much for her—she had not entirely the Norman strength for crime. All his life he would see that thin figure clothed in black, except for the white nunlike wimple that made her face look muddy and showed mercilessly the red rims of her eyes. Her shoulders were hunched, like Foulke's, not from deformity, but from huddling in prayer. He could see her in the dark chapel praying, while the chaplain from Kells galloped through the service.

"The children of the Hebrews spread their garments in the way and cried, saying: 'Hosanna to the Son of David: blessed is he that cometh in the name of the Lord.'"

"Let this mind be in you," the priest read from the Psalter, "which was also in Christ Jesus: who, being in the form of God, thought it not robbery to be equal with God: but made himself of no reputation, and took upon him the form of a servant."

"Unrighteous witnesses are come about me," shrilled the small acolyte, ". . . but thou, O Lord, my defender, maintain my cause."

"For trouble is at hand and there is none to help me."

"But thou, O Lord, my defender, maintain my cause."

His uncle Foulke, Miles noticed, paid no attention to the service, but sat studying a problem of geometry, while Miles' mother knelt huddling a large gold cross to her breast. Foulke never even rose when the hymn was sung: "*Vexilla regis prodeunt*," "The Royal

Banners Forward Go," but his cold eye swept the files of pike- and bow-men and castle servants as they stood rank by rank and howled the hymn. And Miles pondered how his mother, who in all outward seeming and in observance of ritual, was a saint, could half-starve the outside servants, and drive dreadful bargains with hucksters, and throw a poor, seduced Norman girl, some months short of her time, out in the road, to the charity of the wandering Irish smiths. And yet there she knelt huddled in adoration.

"All my brethren removed afar off from me, and mine acquaintance, as though they were strangers, have departed from me," went on the service.

"My lovers and my neighbours,"

"As though they were strangers have departed from me."

"All my brethren afar off from me, and mine acquaintance, as though they were strangers have departed from me," was repeated.

"Deliver my soul, O God, from the peril of the sword," the priest prayed.

"And my darling," shrilled the acolyte, "from the power of the dog."

CRUSADE

II

Though the house seemed to think of
nothing but politics and the possibility of
war, and of religion, yet life began for young
Miles the instant he left the atmosphere of the
house. There was in his heart, unknown to
mother or uncles, a love for this country, for
the reeded banks of the Liffey, for the blue
mountains and fields. Rowan trees and
larch trees and the hazel boughs, heavy with
fruit; and wind raising the unsheaved barley,
and calling the tongue ferns out of dumbness;
the glossy ravens stalking over newly-ploughed
land, rich as and coloured like plums: the
crying of lambs in April, the belled heather,
the sunburnt corn, the vast Hunter's Moon,
all these seemed to have a deep Irishness.
The rising of the trout at dawn; the grazing
of snipe, grazing as cattle do, in the bogs at
night; the storm-driven moon, the badger
hurrying home at daylight, the badger like a
toy-bear. He was sure no other country had
all these things. The Irish cared for them.
The Normans did not. He wondered how
the English felt. They were a quiet people,
who had had bad luck. Harried and con-

quered by Pict and Scot and Roman and Dane
and Norman, all the English wanted was
quiet, to plant their corn and tend their
sheep. A peaceable people and kind-hearted!
The Irish were neither peaceable nor kind-
hearted, but they were alive, as the Normans
weren't. But their life was a mystery. They
had a sort of dark, hidden life, all their own.
Their names for the stars were mystical. The
Milky Way of the Norman was the Ear of
Wheat to the Gael. Orion's Belt was the
Blue Lance of Angus. There were stars
whose names he knew in Irish that were
unknown in Norman speech. The Doe Leap-
ing, the Gleaner, the Twin Breasts of Grania.
When the Normans saw the Northern lights
across the sky, they called it the Polar Dawn
but the Irish called it the Spears of Fionn.
Swift to anger, offended by hardly noticeable
gesture or small, clumsy word—swift to take
sides in a quarrel, and swifter even to change
sides, they were loyal to something within
them, something powerfully racial, not to
one another, but to some heady, turbulent
spirit of the Gael. Young Miles loved their
affection for horse and hound and man. The
affection for horse and dog never changed,

but the affection for a man might change
overnight to a savage, unreasoning hatred.
You never knew where you were with his
father's folk. Their mind would start off
racing at a tangent, so swiftly you didn't even
know the direction it had taken. What Irish
clans he saw did not impress him. Sometimes out of Connemara, or the Woods of
Fermanagh, or Monaghan of the Bogs, an
Irish chieftain would come to the Curragh of
Kildare for the racing. A king, he would call
himself, and insist on kingly honours. He
would be cloaked in saffron and have great
saffron dogs and his harpist with him.
Wherever they sat down, the harpist would
unsling his instrument and begin on a poem
of praise of his master, more intricate in
technique than any tenzon or alba of the
troubadours, more musical than the little songs
of Flanders, and yet—such arrant rubbish:

" *Do bhrigh gur Phœnix e agas morflaith,*
Cloch don chriostail is glaine san Euroip,
Carbuncail gan duibhe iona croine—
Ri-laoch, ri-sheabhac, ri-cheann conndae."

"For the reason that he is a Phœnix and a
great Prince, a gem of the clearest crystal in

Europe, a carbuncle without darkness or discolourment—king-hero, king-hawk, king-head of a county!"

When the effusion was finished, the king in the saffron cloak, the shaggy saffron dogs, and the saffron-faced harpist sat down together and scratched for fleas. No wonder the Normans laughed. The Normans laughed no more, for a laugh meant a knife in the gullet, and that meant the massacre of the Irish in question, and that entailed generations of cattle-raiding and murder. But still, the whole thing was ridiculous. Of course, all the Irish regal families were not like that. The O'Neills, O'Conors, O'Morchas were different, but they weren't quite modern. As a boy he had often thought of riding into Ulster to his father's people. But his father's people, he resented, had never shown any sign of interest in him, and the estate in County Down was in the possession of his father's brother, Eamonn Gorv, or Edmond the Rough. The O'Neills looked on him as a Fitzpaul. And even if he did go up there, young Miles thought, and were accepted as a son of the sept, what was there for him? He would have to fall in with a life of short, savage wars, of hunting, of gambling for herds of cattle at chess, of drinking the heavy malted spirits of Ulster. His father had revolted against that life and come to Lucan. If his father could not stand that kind of existence, how much less could he!

And yet he could not acknowledge himself as Norman. Something revolted against it. Once his mother had found him talking Erse to a servant. She stopped. Her lips closed to the tightness of her purse's mouth.

"I did not know you spoke the Irish jargon," she said in a voice cold as a Norman winter.

"Of course I speak the Erse tongue, Madame," Miles answered pleasantly.

Her eyes had a cold light in them, like the light of swords.

"Why do you not call me 'Mother'?"

"If you distinctly wish it, I shall, of course, Madame."

She hurried off to the chapel.

In the house his uncles were beginning to regard him with a flattering suspicion. They were beginning to fear the Irish in him. On one occasion they were coldly furious. The

Abbot of Clonmacnoise, a thin, saintly-faced Englishman of Lancaster, was visiting Lucan, when Foulke presented his nephew as Milo Fitzpaul.

"My Uncle Foulke must be distracted a little, Lord Abbot," Miles gave his disarming laugh, "but my name is O'Neill, and my baptismal name is not Milo, but Miles, in the Gaelic tongue, Maelmorra, or servant of Mary."

The old Englishman looked at him keenly.

"Do names mean so much to you, my son?"

"My Uncle Foulke," Miles smiled, "has imbued me with a passion for exactness."

It was this incident, he often thought later, which led to his coming to Palestine. There must have been many consultations between the two brothers and their sister. Then the Abbot of Kells sent for him.

"Why Miles," he wheezed, "now you are man-big, have you ever thought what would become of you?"

"Often, sir."

"Have you thought of the possibility of getting your father's estate in Ulster?"

"I'm afraid there's very little chance."

The Abbot fingered the silver cord around his white robe. "Are you sure of that?" he asked.

"Quite sure."

"So am I. But I didn't know you were. Now as to Lucan, I suppose you understand that when your father, God have——" the Abbot stopped, the cold eye of young Miles having caught his as a sword—"when your father left it"—the Abbot took up—"it was not one twentieth the value it is now. That nineteen parts of value of twenty belongs to your Uncle Foulke, to dispose of as he wishes, because he has invested his money and brains in it, at your mother's wish. Do you deny that?"

"What use could there be in denying it?"

"None, my boy, none at all. But I had not looked to see such good sense in you. Now as to what you may expect at your Uncle Foulke's death, I will tell you: nothing. Less than nothing. Your Uncle Foulke is a maniac on the Fitzpaul family. You don't give a dog's bark for all the Fitzpauls, living or dead, do you? Speak out," he urged, "I'm only your old uncle."

"Old Uncle," Miles laughed, "listen." He whistled a bar. "I don't care that,"

"My God!" chuckled the Abbot, "but what a pleasure it is to talk to you! Now. as to your mother's share of the estate, and as to all your mother's money, I fear," he pondered, "I fear it will go to the church."

"Uncle Hugues," young Miles asked, "what of my share?"

"It will take a long time to settle," the Abbot was bland. "These lawyers!"

"Now I know where I am," young Miles nodded.

"And now that you know where you are," Uncle Hugues had waited an instant, "had you decided on any plan or design of life? You needn't tell me, Miles, if you don't wish to. Good God, I am all for liberty, abbot though I am!"

Miles thought. Yes, he had one thought often in his mind, and that was to join with the Geraldines—not the Dublin branch, but the Fitzgeralds of Glyn, who were holding the Shannon against the Connemara tribes, or the younger branch in the south, in Kerry that was like Portugal, so travellers said, in tree and mountain, in beast and flower. A fabled land of lakes and skies bluer than the sea, and the tribes there were the survivors of the disaster when great Atlantis sank like a leaking vessel into the engulfing deep. He liked the Geraldines, but he couldn't join them. After all, his mother was a Fitzpaul, and enemy as he was to the family, he could not make friends with the family enemies. If he did he knew that were the fortunes of the Fitzpauls to turn and Clangarrett, as the Irish called the Geraldines, prevail, Lucan would be his. But he could not do it. There were things which a man of standards couldn't bring himself to do.

"I suppose," he told the Abbot, "that the best thing for me to do is to hire out as under-officer, ensign, or at the worst file-commander to some captain in the Low Countries, or on the Rhine. War is the only chance for the poor man." He laughed. "I am a bit of a philosopher, Uncle Hugues."

"What would you say," Uncle Hugues leaned forward and looked at him, "if I were to send you to England and have you knighted by the English king, and furnish you with an equipment equal to any cadet's of a great family, and find you a commander in the wars?"

"In England?"

"Ah, no," the Abbot was firm, "not so near home as that. I thought of sending you with Ulick de Lacy to the Holy Land."

"The Holy Land?"

"Heart of God! Boy! Cannot you see what an opportunity that is? Once again Europe has got a throwing hold on Asia. Do you think we shall stop at Acre and Jerusalem? With Araby the Fortunate and the Yemen with its houses rooved with gold to be taken and held? Lord God! If I were young again it is not a principality of the Church at which I should aim, but a principality of Arabia." And the man's shabby eyes blazed with old magnificence.

"Well, do you accept or do you not, Miles?" His eyes were shrewd again.

"The Irish part of me, Uncle Hugues, says: 'go to hell, and take your charity with you.' But the Norman part accepts."

"The Norman spirit that hears adventure calling!"

"Not at all," the nephew said, "The Norman spirit that sees a profit in something. The Norman shrewdness that tells me if I can't get what I want, to take what I can get."

"And what a pleasure it will be for your poor mother," purred the Abbot of Kells, "to think she has a son fighting for Holy Cross in the Holy Land!"

III

If he had had the choice, young Miles thought, he would not have chosen for chieftain this red-faced, blustering, drinking man. But after being with him on the long march through France to the harbour of Hyères, and on the long voyage to Jaffa, he was forced to admit that Ulick de Lacy was a fine soldier. He drank too much, but never until he saw his men disposed for the night, all present and correct and sentries set. And in the morning, he was there to see that everything was in order. The Irish clansmen adored him. As it was the man was born a century too late. When the first Normans came to Ireland he would have been in his element, a roystering raider living on the Irish country, as now his intent was to live on Palestine. There were pilgrims to be accompanied and protected to the Holy Places from Jaffa, at so much a head, like sheep. Already in Europe there was deep feeling against the Templars, and many an abbot of other orders, and many a foreign baron and princeling would as little put himself under their protection as under the protection of Satan's self. Also, their rule for pilgrims was too strict. So twenty bands like de Lacy's were functioning and thriving in the Holy Land. Also many a potentate, whose lease of territory was from de Bouillon's time, needed either help in holding it or in getting into possession. There was big money to be made there, too. Moreover, de Lacy had a kinsman who was Prior of the Temple in Syrian Tripoli, so that here he had an advantage over the other free lances in Palestine. He was glad to have young Miles O'Neill along, for he pitied a little and admired a great deal the young knight. O'Neill was impeccably bred, whereas though de Lacy's sire was beyond reproach, his dam, as he himself confessed, was a bit of a mystery. He had also the rough man's awe before education. O'Neill could read and write. God's Knees! that was wonderful. He was never tired of talking about his young lieutenant.

"This Holy Land was just made for us, my boy," he would thunder. "You've got breeding and brains, and I've got ambition and a few other things." He would bring his hand, heavy as a mallet, on young Miles' shoulder. "Leave it to me. Not for nothing have I a strain of travelling pedlar in me." Poor, big-hearted, wrong-headed de Lacy!

When all arrangements for their patrol were made and the route laid out—Jaffa to Lydda, past Rama, and from Lydda the long thirty miles to Jerusalem, de Lacy began to show a genius for organisation that made young Miles O'Neill laugh. He bought forty donkeys and put them in charge of a Maronite Christian, with instructions to say they were his own and to demand a certain sum for their hire. The pilgrims, who had heard that everything was cheap in the Holy Land, wept in impotent anger, but de Lacy was sympathetic. Their gratitude was boundless when the big Norman with loud shouts and crackings of his whip obtained some small reduction. It spoiled for them the pleasant ride through the plains of thyme and hyssop, through the fields of cotton and past the orchards of fig and apricot trees. At Lydda, the same comedy of hiring camels was enacted, and thence onward the march was painful and dangerous, grey mountains with vast boulders which a child's hand might send down on the caravan. Here it was O'Neill's work to ride ahead with a picked party of mountainy Irish and see that no Arab party was lurking amid the great stones. Miles was always glad to get ahead, for the pilgrims bored him. They came to Palestine with tales of marvels in their ears, of monsters in the desert half goat and half man; of the phœnix with its tail barred gold, silver, and diamond; of fowls with wool instead of feathers; of trees that yield honey, meal, and poison—in fine, they believed every foolish tale that a wandering palmer or unfrocked Minorite had ever told to get a lodging for the night. They believed that on the other side of the Dead Sea was the country of Ghengis Khan. De Lacy, while not quite allowing them to believe everything, hinted at stories he could tell of Trans-Jordania. De Lacy had arrangements with merchants of relics, who sold beads and crosses to his caravan, made of the olive trees of Mount Olivet, so they claimed, or of terebinth, the tree under which the Virgin rested when she was carrying Christ to be presented in the

Temple; small round stones called Cornioli, to expel poison; the Eagle's stone, called Aquilina, which ensures the easy birth of children; also, Girdles of Mary, made of Bethlehem shells, whose virtues are sworn to be miraculous and many. There was no alley down which the big wheezing Leinster-man would not chase a sequin of gold. Also, did a foreign baron find the pilgrimage begin to pall on him, he could always have a night's gaming. This was de Lacy's passion. When he won, he won gallantly; when he lost, he played like a fool. He would follow bad luck as though it were his best friend. After a spell of it, the donkey-hire at Jaffa would rise to unheard of prices. But the big man had virtues outstanding his mean traits. When a pilgrim was under his protection, his life was as safe as could humanly be assured. There were ugly stories in the Holy Land of patrol leaders whose caravans had been robbed by Arabians with whom an arrangement had been made, or by Arabians who were not Arabians at all, but ruffian Christians in Arab dress. De Lacy was not of those against whom a scandal of this kind could be told.

But the escorting of pilgrims was but a pretext in de Lacy's mind for remaining in the Holy Land. He wanted greater prizes. Light wars and ransoms. His opportunity came when a claimant to the manor of Bethlehem came out of Poland, a third cousin of the holder. It was a curious and unsound claim. The seigneurie had been conferred on a Polish noble by the third Baldwin for his bravery in the retreat from Damascus. The Polander had married a Moslem neighbour's daughter after her formal baptism. His son was lax in mind, as half-breeds are, and when he succeeded his father, married a Moslem, in this generation without the formality of baptism. In the third generation, the seigneurie was once more Mohammedan, although the holder was a subject of the King of Jerusalem. But the King of Jerusalem was now Emperor of Germany, having married John de Brienne's daughter, and the Emperor was under interdict from the Pope. The Arabian sultan of Syria and Palestine was Cohreddin, who was all for peace, and to whom the arrangement of a seigneur of Bethlehem who had professed Islam was welcome. When the cousin out of Poland, Andreas Lallemant, appeared to state his case, there was none before whom he could lay it. His contention was that his ancestor had been granted the fief for Christian valour. The present holder was a Moslem. Therefore the holder's claim was null. And he, next of kin in a direct line, should have it. The patriarch of Jerusalem was as much for peace as the Sultan. Besides, Bethlehem was not important strategically. So long as Christians visited the Church in peace he did not care who held ownership. Andreas appealed to the Grand Master of the Templars. The Grand Master was sympathetic, but what could the Templars do? It was a question for the Emperor. But the Emperor was notedly pro-Saracen. The Grand Master was afraid that any action must be by Andreas' self. Had he any friends in the Holy Land? Did he know any of the free knights who could give him advice? Sir Fynes Sambourne? Sir John Ixley? Sir Ulick de Lacy, the cousin of the Prior of Tripoli? A fine knight, that latter—the Grand Master smiled—a burly, hot-headed man.

De Lacy listened to the Polish nobleman with a judicial quiet. "You wish to get this renegade cousin of yours out? You wish my advice? God's Wounds! Kick him out!"

"But how?"

"Have you any money?"

He had a thousand zecchins—

"It's little! It's little!" De Lacy pondered. "But when you are Lord of Bethlehem and Warden of the Manger, you will not forget the guileless old soldiers who have helped you get your rights. Pass it over."

"But—"

"Pass it over! I have taken a vast liking to you, and I cannot bear to see you wronged. I have probably been described to you as a cold, inactive man, but Cross of God! my heart boils to think that a slippered Saracen bastard should shuffle it in the halls where your sainted great uncle's heels have rung. No! Not nine hundred! The whole thousand, if you please!" He went and saw it counted and weighed. "And now—"

"And now?" The Polander did not seem quite happy.

"And now, go and have your claim indited in flowery language and a fine clerkly hand, and send it in ten days—not sooner, mark you, to your cousin in Bethlehem. Tell him to give up the fief, or that you and your friends will take it from him!"

"What will he do?" asked Andreas

"Laugh his head off," chuckled de Lacy.

There was a good deal of the prophet in the wheezing Leinsterman. The Mohammedan cousin, taking the claim for what it was, worthless, and taking the threat of armed force as one of the braggart vows common in Palestine at the time, kicked the Pole's messenger out. He had him tied facing his donkey's rump, and hunted out of the small town for presumption. The wretched herald was hardly out of sight of the Bethlehemites when de Lacy struck. He had enlisted an hundred English bowmen and a half-dozen Teutonic knights to support him and his Irish command. They swarmed into Bethlehem like a crowd of locusts. Within half-an-hour Bethlehem was de Lacy's, at the cost of ten men. He rounded up the renegade Lallemant, a quiet pale young Saracen, and his children and womenfolk.

"So you have accepted Islam," laughed de Lacy. "We will now see what your Saracen friends will do for you. Your wife is a daughter of the Ameer Yussuf. I think there's about seven thousand gold pieces in this lot. I promised you solid money, young O'Neill."

"De Lacy," O'Neill looked keenly at him, "you are my officer, and when you fight, I fight. I'm not sure Lemon-face," he nodded at the Polish knight, "has any title here. But I know this: all you've contracted to do is to make this poor devil give up possession. If you hold the family now to ransom, you are doing an unwise thing."

"Getting seven thousand pieces of Damascus is not unwise."

"De Lacy, we may swing for it."

"As if all of us, my boy, didn't risk our necks every week here." De Lacy chuckled. "Not our necks, I'll grant, but our skins for a few lousy pilgrims' sous. I'll risk my neck cheerfully for seven thousand gold zecchins."

The women were terrified, huddling together, but the children had ceased sobbing since Miles began to speak. The young Saracen's face might have been carved out of burned earth, so little interest did it show. The mouth still held the slight smile of scorn.

"It will be unlucky money," Miles urged, knowing de Lacy's weak spot. "You would lose it the first big game you went into. O Ulick of my heart," he changed into Gaelic speech, "is it in your mind to give up this place to that scabby Dantzic rat?"

"It is not in my mind," de Lacy laughed.

"Then, for God's sake, give the man on the wrong side of the bargain his luck-money and let him go."

"He'll be back in a week with his wife's people."

"They'll be here, anyway."

"All right, let them go." Miles began to explain in Arabic they were free. "But look you, young O'Neill, don't give them the best the stable has, or you'll talk to me."

The sallow Polander raised shrill protest when he saw the prisoners depart. "Are you for letting them go?"

"What else?" said de Lacy dangerously.

"But couldn't we keep his wife? As a hostage?"

"Ha! He takes us for women-dealers, this one!" de Lacy cursed him terribly. "And now, you! In a week there'll be fighting here, savage, wolves' fighting. You must go at once to the Emperor at Brundusium, and tell him what you have done. Frederick has the right to certify you in your holding. But before you go, you must get your writer to give me and my lieutenant O'Neill authority to hold this place for you. And you will say that we do it only out of Christian zeal, and urged to it by you."

"You do it for nothing?"

"Not a brown penny in it for us."

"Then I shall write it at once, and start at once."

"Won't you wait for the fighting?" asked de Lacy.

"I think it most important to put the case before the Emperor as quickly as possible."

"If he goes to Frederick," de Lacy told Miles, "we shall never see him again. No, never again."

"Because of what, de Lacy?"

"Because," de Lacy roared his most shattering laugh, "because the Magnificence will hang him."

CHAPTER IV

DE LACY was silent as he went his rounds.
De Lacy drank no wine. In his moonlike
face his eyes became pin-pricks. He whistled
tunelessly as he examined each door and wall.
He called to Miles and went with him for a
walk around the castle. He measured the
place, pacing his steps. He turned to Miles.

"Did you say that Arab had the wrong side
of the bargain?"

Miles looked at him in surprise

"You're a good judge of a man and a good
judge of a horse, Miles, and you've got the
technic of a captain-general, but, my God!
boy! Can't you see this place is not built
for war? God's Face! We're done." He
put a hand on Miles' shoulder.

"We'll fight outside, then."

"We'll have to," de Lacy agreed. "Even
at that, we're between cavalry and a wall.

I'll drop into Jerusalem and see if we can't get some help."

While he was gone, Miles scented around to see if there were any way of erecting a hampering barrier of stones, knowing as he did that Arab horses could not jump, but the terrain was too wide. One could not tell from what angle the Arab would strike. He had to content himself with placing bowmen and kerns, uncertain even if he had placed them right, but trusting for the best. The Teutoric knights were stupid and useless. Every detail of food and water O'Neill had to supervise himself. At midnight de Lacy clattered back.

"Any luck?"

"Curse them!" De Lacy was coldly furious. "Moral support and talk of high politic. At any rate, there's this: it will be a family quarrel for the present. The Sultan of Damascus won't meddle—

"Miles," he said suddenly, "after all this isn't your fight. I asked in Jerusalem if the Temple wouldn't let you go through Palestine in the robes of the order. And they will. From Jaffa you can take ship to Cyprus—"

"Thanks, de Lacy. But I won't leave you and the Irish men."

"You know," the big man worried, "if Cohreddin gets us into Damascus we'll be beheaded as lousy pirates. As to me, the Sultan would be right. But you're different."

"I'm not going, de Lacy. And we haven't lost yet. We've got to keep the men cheerful."

"All right, Miles. Let's go the rounds."

On the fourth day the Arabs struck. They galloped down with dawn. They came quietly like ghosts on horseback, like threatening ghosts on fleet horses. There was not enough light for effective archery and before the bowmen could form into files of pikes so as to withstand the assault, the Arabs were in, slashing and backhanding with their double-edged Damascus swords, keen as razors. De Lacy was everywhere, an unassailable tower of defence. His terrible boring charge and heavy battle-axe swept every knot down. But the bowmen were retreating. It was then that O'Neill gave the loud cry of "Red Hand!" and that the kerns, mad for fighting, leaped at the horsemen with their long knives.

CRUSADE

They pulled the Saracen out of the saddle. They hacked and thrust half cursing, half sobbing, until the unaccustomed battle, as with mad dogs, put a panic on horses and horsemen. Sunlight shot up from the East like a lighted beacon, and the archers, re-forming under their Yorkshire sergeant, began to find the range. Twang! Hiss! Thud! And suddenly the white, ghostly company faded off, with the soft drumming of their mounts' unshodden hoofs.

II

O'Neill knew, when he dragged the big Turk from his horse and hit him that savage backhander with the edge of his flattened mailed right hand on the burly neck, that he had killed the man, but in the instant afterward, when a rider had swung a mace at his own head, he was sure he too was dead. He had dropped into a gulf of blackness. And now he was swimming with incredible pain and weariness, through an oily trough of pain and weariness into life again. He tried to lift his head, but felt it a jagged star of agony. He tried to lift his left hand to it. He felt the shoulder move, but the arm did not respond. He knew his arm was broken.

The sun, like molten brass, poured into his eyes when he opened them. He closed them again and listened. There was no shouting, no nervous treading of horses. The fight was over then. And de Lacy had lost it, or Miles would not be lying there in the cruel Asian sun. He wondered if de Lacy had escaped.

He had felt somehow that morning that he was not going to die. Something told him that he would emerge from the fight alive. But de Lacy, he knew, had felt he would never see Miles again. They had, in the ghostly hours before dawn, laid out their plans of battle, tactically occupying the top of the gorge through which they knew the Damascene riders were coming. De Lacy had given his last instructions, and Miles was walking off with a "See you after it, Ulick!" when de Lacy went after him and put an arm around him:

"Miles, avick," he said, "could you find it in you to forgive me for bringing you here?" His wide gesture embraced all Asia.

CRUSADE

"I can never thank you enough, de Lacy. Stop fretting. I'm all right."

"I trust to God you are."

"If I were as sure about you," Miles said, "as about myself. Listen, Ulick, don't take your helmet off and fight bareheaded. You under-rate those Saracen archers. And that red poll of yours is a mark in a hundred."

"Good luck to you, boy!"

They had known, after that first attack in Bethlehem, that the Saracen would come again, and come again in sufficient force. Whatever policy was behind Cohreddin's inaction, the Sultan of Damascus was not going to let his brethren in the faith be slaughtered without reprisal. In Jerusalem, de Lacy had learned through the Templar spies that the raid they had beaten off was led by the Ameer Yussuf himself, one of the crack cavalry leaders of Trans-Jordania, the uncle of the outraged lord of Bethlehem. The Templars were delighted with the result of the fight, but still could not meddle. Some of the knights of Mount Joye, however, offered to come in with de Lacy. Somewhence O'Neill's commander got money, and an hundred and fifty more men.

"If there were anything to defend, they'd be a good lot," de Lacy mused. He took O'Neill aside. "I've got an idea, Miles. This crowd in Jerusalem," he nodded backward, "are too fixed in their ideas of warfare. Give them something like Mount Joye or Acre to defend and only sickness and famine will beat them. Or give them a game of chess with companies of troops in the field. We haven't got anything to defend, and we have damned few men. My Miles, we have got to use our heads."

The big man may have looked stupid and heavy to the Templars, but he knew what he was about. He had scented in the air, and from the Templars' petulance, that some treaty of accord was being drawn up with the Emperor—the Second Frederick, who was Arab in all but birth and profession of creed. Cohreddin would not meddle in the Bethlehem fight as a Moslem prince, he knew. The peace loving Mohammedan would hardly imperil the unsigned agreement. But he would send unofficial help. That the unofficial help would be forthcoming within ten days he knew. If de Lacy could defeat the next raid heavily, Cohreddin might let him remain in possession, the Polish knight could be "handled," even if the Emperor did not hang him. If the worst came to the worst the Saracen owner would ransom the fief handsomely. But first the forces from Damascus must be beaten.

He had an idea, de Lacy said, picked up from the Irish and Scottish wars. If, instead of waiting to be attacked, they attacked first, in this manner; by ambushing the Saracens. They would come up naturally from the old seigneurie of Kerak, skirting the Dead Sea, through Zoara and Carmel and Saint Abraham.

"Now, listen," he told Miles, "the Templars have their spies everywhere. A runner on a racing dromedary will let us know when they are coming. The heavy crowd I'll keep with me—bowmen and pikes, and the few knights. I'll give them sweet hell for a while and then I'll fall back. You know what the Arabs are when you start staggering. They go in to finish you. Then you'll come in."

"Where'll I be?" Miles asked.

"You'll be quietly on the hillside, out of sight, behind the boulders. When we've got a good block of them in the gorge, you and some of the Irish troops will start rolling the boulders down on them, following it up with a pike charge. The crowd behind will bolt. When we've got them nicely, I'll turn. By God! Miles!" he swore, "I believe we'll beat the Sultan our two selves. Now leg up, and we'll look over the ground. You want a work party to cut olive clubs for levering the rocks."

On the seventh day a Templar brother came to tell them that black tents were pitched in Tophila, and that the gathering seemed mostly Bedouin—the usual unit of two Bedouins to one camel, one to ride and one to lead, and both to fire with light bows from behind the kneeling beast. They were evidently, said the Templar brother, waiting for cavalry from Damascus, and Bostra, and Jerash.

"No! Not really!" de Lacy murmured politely.

A day later a Bedouin rode in to say that the horsemen had arrived and the caravans of camels were starting.

"How many horsemen?" de Lacy asked.

"Many!"

"I said: How many?"

"God damn your black face!" de Lacy was furious. "I should have sent out myself and not trusted these Templar fools."

It occurred to Miles that the Templars were not such fools as it seemed. If there had been a huge force, de Lacy might have retired; above all things the Templars wanted to keep up the tradition of Christian battle. So their spy may have been more knave than fool. No matter, he thought, they'd have to fight now anyway. He cantered off with de Lacy to inspect the terrain. . . .

It seemed to Miles in the hushed, grey morning, as he lay concealed behind his boulder, the small Provençal trumpeter beside him, and watched the Arabs file into the gorge, that everything was not going to be quite as de Lacy had imagined it. First came a troop of horsemen, light cavalry, he could tell by their step, probably armed with lance and scimitar, and after that a great pushing wave of camels. He could hear their groaning in the darkness. How many were there? One hundred? An hundred and fifty? Good God! De Lacy had thought they'd be behind the main body of horse. The gorge would be choked with the wretched beasts. And now there was the jangle of chains—the real body of cavalry. De Lacy must soon be at work. Ah, there went the calls. North of him, he could hear stamping, clatter of steel, the screaming of a frightened mount. Faintly he could hear de Lacy's voice, like the ghost of a voice at that distance. He wondered with a sickly grin what de Lacy would make of those camels! That living rampart was genius! Ha! Holy Cross! If they would only not underrate these Saracens. The early zodiacal light began to throw a ghostly illumination in the gorge. The cloaked riders went on ahead as though nothing were happening. A Saracen scout galloped back alongside of the hill, avoiding the main body, and near enough to Miles to be hit by a thrown pebble. He tore recklessly down the hill. Miles wondered how young Fitz-Gibbon, from Mount Joye, was standing the strain on the other side of the gorge.

He waited for as long as he could count five hundred, expecting every instant a runner from de Lacy to tell him what was going on at the mouth of the valley. There seemed to be a great shouting, and now the shouting grew less loud. And all the time beneath him the river of horsemen flowed. How many were there? The green light faded into grey, grey of a cat, and there was already, or perhaps he only imagined it, a faint blush of rose in the east. The gaunt rocks of Hebron began to take ghostly, threatening shapes. He could wait no longer.

"Give her a blow, boy!" he told the trumpeter.

The golden hunting call soared over the grim grey valley. At the second bar the boulders began to fall. There was a sort of chink as great stone struck small stone on its way downward. Miles could hear the men grunting as they hove the levers of olive wood. There was a rustle as the stone began rolling, like the rustle some great reptile might make as it went over dry ground. Then a thudding as of some vast playing ball as it hit the ground from a hurling stick. FitzGibbon's piper began his mad shrilling.

"Pikes short! Under the armpit!" Miles ordered. "Don't run. Quick walk!"

He felt, swinging down the hillside, his feet timing to the distant pipes, that there was some vast mistake about all this. That the dim hosting below him was a hosting of shades. There had been no screaming, no panic, such as he and de Lacy had imagined. He would not be surprised, he thought, if when he would hit a man of them, his blade went through air. There was talk in Ireland by the firesides of riders who rode by night from the great burial ground of Tallaght to the strand of the Irish sea—the cavalry of dead Parthelon, from Carthage or perhaps Atlantis: who knew!—and Danish and Norman patrols who had set to receive their charge had felt only a wind blowing over them as from the snowy mountains at the Pole.

"MacHugh O'Hara!" he called to the ensign of the pikes, "Make your men scatter out! They're clumping."

Then the sun rose.

There was in his ears the tweeting of birds —apart from the skirl of the pipes, he could hear them. The miracle of light came. It came down from the blue sky like a rich transparent wine. The last stars guttered. Across the gorge he could see FitzGibbon's men trotting like dogs. He felt their teeth were bared, like wolf-dog's teeth. High on the hill the piper strutted, his kilt flirting like the tail of a bird. Then Miles looked down.

They sat like rocks on their glossy horses. They sat with their heads and faces muffled in their black cloaks, with their right arms free. Their blades were upright in their hands. In the very quietness of them there was the threat of doom. They were like the heads of snakes, raised to strike. He looked down the gorge to the south. Everywhere black cloaks and bared swords.

"Are you ready, O'Hara?"

"We're ready, captain of my heart."

O'Neill chose three runners. The men came with unwillingness. It needed a sharp word to take them from the fight.

Toward the south, O'Neill could see the Arabs coming in a sweeping fan-like movement up each side of the gorge. They were trapped. The ensign was looking impatiently at his men. O'Neill looked at him.

"Good-bye, O'Hara."

"Good-bye, Captain," the ensign smiled. "Pikes! Ready! Full shaft! Go!'

They wouldn't last a half-hour, O'Neill feared. He saw that the Arabs leader had drawn back his men from the clutter of dead men and horses and great stones, and that these were a sort of rampart for them. He saw the pikes on each side begin to climb. Then the Arab cavalry charged.

He watched the troops galloping up from the southward, the fan-like movement was turning in, like the horns of the moon. High over the screaming and the cursing the piper was piping away.

"You will get back to the Sieur de Lacy somehow," he told the runners, "and tell him from me that there is no hope; that I put the Saracen at not less than fifteen hundred men. You will tell him that he must save himself; that there is nothing else to do."

He paused.

"Anything else, sir?"

"Yes. Say Red Hand is happy. Go."

He counted slowly up to twenty. "Go!" he told the second runner, "but keep higher up hill."

He counted up to forty: "Go!" he told the third man, "take the trumpeter with you. No, boy! You must go! Now, off!"

Like a mirage in the desert, it seemed to him, this battle in the gorge below. The savage shouting of the kerns had ceased and he knew now they were in a grim silent struggle for their lives, gaunt, broken-headed men, wielding their pikes as protection. Even the piper's piping had ceased, and O'Neill, looking up to see if he could spot his body, saw that the man was not dead at all. He had flung down bag and reeds and with drawn knife was bounding down the hill to die with his comrades. "Am I the only man left unfighting in this cursed place?" Miles laughed. A loose mount came bounding up the hill, a small black Arab mare. He caught it by the bridle. "You'll do, lady," he said. Under the low authoritative voice, she stood as quietly as at her rack. He pulled his surcoat of chain over his hips, and settled the light helmet on his head, snugged the chain mittens over wrists and backs of hands. Drew his blade and dropped the scabbard to the ground. "Too light!" he thought, taking a trial cut, "I should have brought the other one."

He crossed himself on forehead and breast. "Save me from the lion's mouth, O Lord," he prayed swiftly, "and my lowliness from the horns of the unicorns!" He pivoted into the saddle, set the mare slithering downhill. Before him was a knee-high barricade of dead horses and great stones and dead and wounded men. He slapped the mare with the flat of his blade. "Hip!" he broke her into a canter and set her at it. She took the obstacle by the roots and sent him flying through the air. His light Italian weapon broke off at the hilt as he fell. "I should have remembered these damned Arabs can't jump."

A line of pikemen were rallying after having been pushed back to the barricade. Their mouths were tight lines and their eyes were bitter. He made for them.

"Where's Black MacHugh?"

"He's underneath, captain."

"Where's the Templar knight, Fitz-Gibbon?"

"We don't rightly know, but we think he's underneath too. Look out, Captain."

Three Arab horsemen came driving at them. O'Neill picked up a pike, and slipping to the left, out of reach of the trooper's sword arm, brought his mount down with the shaft between his forelegs. As the rider scrambled to his feet and came rushing at him, O'Neill drove the blade of the pike into his face. A second of the trio was killed by a hulking Kerryman. The third galloped back.

"Come on. Get into a ring," O'Neill directed. "By God! Is there no sense at you at all? Is it children I'm dealing with? Pike out and right knee on ground. We'll get out of this yet."

"If my captain pleases," the huge Kerryman said, "I won't leave this place until I've tallied my dozen."

"Are you all right? Are any of you wounded?"

"We're all right, but our throats are cracked on us."

"'Tis better than your necks," O'Neill said, and they laughed. "Who seems to be chief of the attack?"

"'Tis that big one on the grey horse yonder, captain. 'Tis him that downed FitzGibbon, captain, and has the tricky, inciting head. A great devil, surely."

"I'll have a crack at him," O'Neill decided. He went toward a dead Saracen and picked up his heavy, cleaving blade. "Keep the ring, and bring any others you can find into

it." He walked swiftly toward the horseman. Four Arabs came charging at him.
He waited until they were almost on him, and
ran out at right-angles. Before they could
turn, he was slipping on hands and knees
through the second line.

"Ho! Such-an-one!" he called in Arabic,
and the man turned.

He did not seem an Arab, the big man.
His huge frame, his cruel, bony face, had in
them something of the Tartar men from the
long plains beyond Damascus. He had small,
greenish eyes. His sparse moustaches were
like those of a cat. The great grey horse,
O'Neill noticed, was a Crusader's captured
mount, a great, heavy-boned animal of
Flanders. The Saracen's blade was long and
double edged, and his shield small, round,
and rimmed with studs like an Irish chieftain's. Instead of device, it bore Arabic
lettering, running over it like fleeing lizards.

The big man smiled. He smiled by hard-
ening his eyes, and opening his mouth. His
teeth were sharp and cruelly white, like the
teeth of wolves. His blade hissed over as
O'Neill jumped. Miles could feel the sharp
lash of it, like the lash of a whip on his chain

mail. His own beautifully-timed stroke the
Tartar caught by raising his shield shoulder-
high. Miles felt his steel sink into the shield
as an axe sinks into a tree. He gave a tug.
He could not unloose it. He felt the Tartar
smile above him. The horseman brought
back his blade in a slow sweeping arc.

It seemed to Miles that inside his own
brain another brain was functioning—of itself,
so quickly did it act. He stood, as it were,
outside himself, and watched himself act,
wondering how he did it. He slipped back,
as though slipping a wrestler's hold. He
jumped in again, grasping the horse's right
ear with his left hand and catching its nose
with his right. He gave the head a vicious
twist, kicking savagely at the forelegs. Man
and charger came down in an appalling
clumsy crash.

He waited an instant until the Tartar got
to his feet. The man's right hand went to
his belt for a knife. Before it got there
O'Neill swooped in and caught the Tartar's
right wrist with his left hand. He twisted
the wrist inward. The Tartar bent forward, his neck outstretched like the neck of
a hissing goose. O'Neill brought the edge

of his right hand, like the edge of a sword, down in a savage chop—a bog-fighter's trick, a portion of his head told him. But there you were! There was the huge man, dead as a rabbit.

But he was not done with the big man yet, for as the hulk fell some buckle or metal loop in his belt caught the edge of Miles' soft otterskin shoes and held him as by a ball and chain. He tried to kick himself free, but could not. And now the Arabs who had watched the fight quietly, expecting the Tartar's victory as a certainty, came riding at him. The foremost was a Bedouin chief, brown-black as his native basalt. He swung a light mace as he rode. Queerly O'Neill watched the charge of the horse instead of the weapon. He knew the weapon would strike him, but he felt it unnecessary to be knocked about by the horse.

"Yes," he decided, "that madman is going to barge right into me."

But before the horse struck him the mace did. He flopped forward like a scarecrow boys might kick about. . . .

Through the tossing welter of pain he heard a voice speaking to him in Arabic. It was a clear flute-like voice. "Are you dying?" it said.

He had turned over on his back, his head resting against a stone. He opened his eyes wearily. His questioner was a young man, his face wrapped in his head-dress. O'Neill could see only fair eyebrows, and an eye clear as his own, grey as lake water. Some northerner of the hills.

"I said: Are you dying?"

"I don't know," O'Neill answered. "I don't think so. I'm just badly mauled. Could you give me a drink of water?"

"Did you kill Mansur Khan?" the voice went on. There was something like clear cold water in the young man's voice, like the water of a little stream going over pebbles.

"Oh, the big fellow, do you mean? Yes, I did for him. What about some water?"

The boy did not move. O'Neill saw he was dressed as a Damascene—red shoes, and great baggy breeches of silk; silk shirt sprigged with gold, and coat of rich peach-coloured silk. In his girdle was a dagger with a beautifully chased gold and turquoise hilt. His head-dress was of rich brocade with fringes of gold. A queer thought came into O'Neill's head, that while he thought he was speaking, he was not speaking at all, that he was dumb. A blow on the head did strange things to you.

"Are you a Christian boy?" he said.

"I am an Arab of the Arab." And the slight figure drew itself up proudly. Then O'Neill understood that he wasn't dumb.

"Oh, I'm sorry for having asked you for water," he said wearily. "I didn't know."

"You shall have water," the boy decided, and walked away. O'Neill closed his eyes wearily.

He seemed to wake out of a half-dream to find his face being moistened by a wet cloth, and water poured on the palms of his hands. A little cup of hammered brass was held to his lips. Thank God for the cool water!

"Did you kill, as they say, Mansur Khan with your empty hands?" the cool voice asked.

"I had to," O'Neill said. "I had no weapon." The weakness rode over him like a wave; passed, as a wave passes. He looked at the young Arab. He could see little of his face But his hands he saw; small, white, beautifully kept. Behind him a vast negro stood, with flattened nose and a mouth like an ugly, healed, blue wound. There were barbaric rings of coarse gold in his ears. From his great fat bulk, as of some harridan fish-wife, O'Neill judged him to be an eunuch bought in Jeddah. So the young Arab was but out of the harem, out of his mother's hands. His first fight, perhaps.

"Are my men all dead?"

"No! Many escaped. And your leader and his main body are safe, not in Bethlehem, but in Jerusalem."

"Thank God!"

"And yet you are left hurt here?"

"That is the luck of fighting," O'Neill said. It was wearying to talk. He wished the young Arab would go away and allow him to sleep. He heard faintly the thud of the feet of horses. "May I have some more water?"

There was a mysterious delay. The young Sheykh seemed to be whispering to the black eunuch. He came to O'Neill.

"Will you eat this?"

"But I don't wish to eat anything.'

"Please," the voice insisted, "please eat this." He opened his eyes. It was a piece of thin Arab bread. "After that you will have water." He tasted it. It was salt as the Dead Sea. "I suppose," O'Neill hinted, "there are many ways of killing a man." He wondered how long it would be before the poison began to rack him. The young Arab flushed red with anger; became white as his head-dress.

"There are some customs we have not yet learned from the Christians," he said. His voice was no longer cool. It was cold as the snow of Lebanon. It was withdrawn, far-off. "Give him water, thou!" he told the negro.

O'Neill heard the clatter of horsemen, the jingle of harness, the shuffle of men dismounting. The negro put his dry scaly hand at the back of O'Neill's neck and held the brass pannikin to his lips. O'Neill saw three men before him; an old, very simply dressed man with gravity and authority in his face. A big sinewy Arab was with him, wearing a twisted green pilgrim's turban. There was a slim youth, who looked like the old man's squire.

"What is this?" the old man asked.

"This is my prisoner, father of Ali," the young Arab stood up before the old sheykh.

"Did you not know," the old man's voice was grave, "that no prisoners are taken this day? That is a compact."

"This is the knight," the young man said, "who killed Mansur Khan with naught in his hands."

"Did you kill Mansur Khan?" the second Arab, the big, fighter-looking man asked.

"If I didn't," O'Neill answered shortly, "there has been a grievous mistake." The big Arab smiled.

"Also there is bread and salt between this man and me," said the young Arab. "And he is my prisoner."

"O sister of Ali!" the old man turned. "What mad thing hast thou done this day?"

It was all like some Italian mummer's play to O'Neill, or some dream a man might have lying in the open under the mad rays of the moon. "Look at me," O'Neill called. "I am no woman's prisoner. O you who spoke," he appealed to the big Arab, "I am not so wounded as I seem. Help me to my feet and lend me a sword and we will finish it, you and

I. It would be very honourable of you."
But the big Arab shook his head.

"Sir," he appealed to the old man, "surely
in war no woman can take a man prisoner."

"We are the Bani Iskander," the old
sheykh answered, "free of all custom and of
every tribute save yearly a sword and a spray
of almond blossom to the Commander of the
Faithful. Among us a woman may be ad-
mitted to the Council of Sheykhs, and what
one sheykh of the Children of Alexander
does, the others abide and are bound by.
You are the prisoner of the sister of Ali."

"Curse the sister of Ali!" O'Neill cried.
His eyes and her eyes met in a duel of anger.
The head-dress had fallen from about her
face, and even in his pain and shame he was
surprised to see the classic Greek beauty of
her features—the straight nose and small clean
mouth of northern folk. So the children of
Alexander the Great were not a myth, like
so many tales that are told, part of his
head thought, while the rest of his brain
seethed with anger. "Ho, fighter!" he appealed to the big Arab, "I will not be a
damned woman's prisoner."

The old man was fumbling at his beard.

"O sister of Ali," he asked, "for how much wilt thou sell this prisoner?"

O'Neill looked at her. What a fool he was to have taken her for a boy. She was only a slight young girl, slight, fine as a young almond tree. She spoke very quietly to the old man.

"O father of Ali," she said, "if he were of any worth I would give him to you. But from me it would be a gift which insults. I sell him for a copper piastre."

"And I buy him, sister of Ali."

The big Arab lieutenant came out and bent over Miles, felt his chest, ran his hands over him until he found the broken left arm. "Akh!" he said in sympathy. He looked at the wound in the hand, trying to slip off the chain mail. "O uncle Haroun," he told the old sheykh, "we need a litter and a physician here." He slid his arm around O'Neill's shoulders and helped him to sit up. "O young man," he half whispered, "thank the sister of Ali for her bread and salt. But for that, of a certainty you would have felt the headsman's sword."

O'Neill felt a sickening sense of shame go through him. And he had suggested she was poisoning him. . . . He looked toward her. She was standing by the old man, talking to him, her light leather whip rapping the ankles of her red boots. Beside the old man, heavy with years and wisdom, she seemed so young, she gave the sense of the spirit of youth, like the young moon the Jews blessed when its thin blade hovered in the west, or like the flash of silver on the blossoming pear-tree.

"O sister of Ali," he said, "I did not understand. I thank you for bread and salt."

She turned to him. Once more the headdress was adjusted around her shoulders, and behind the folds of brocade small firm mouth and small firm chin were withdrawn like a garden behind walls. He could only see the grey eyes smiling at him, and her voice came, gentle as the little bell of Mass.

"It is nothing." And then the eyes grew cold, hard as ice, and the voice had the cut of a Bedouin whip. "Each day I give more to the lepers outside Damascus' wall."

CHAPTER V

I

HE found himself, now that he was aiding the Cornish knight, Trelawney, a figure of importance in Jerusalem. Though the Kentish boy, Josselyn, had not known his name, it was because he was recently over from England. But the Templars and the heavy Germanic knights insisted that he should be henceforth the hero of Rouge Garde, as the gully near Saint Abraham was called. Mansur Khan, Cohreddin's turcoman leader, was well known to the knights of Irak, and there was increasing wonder at the man who had killed him. "If I had been told he was as dangerous as all that," O'Neill commented quite truthfully, "I'd have let him alone." But everyone insisted this was only modesty; only "his gay Irish way." His position now was chief aide to the Cornishman, doing everything, from drilling troops to gathering information as to landing places, and marking routes.

Trelawney was a fat, quiet man, great-framed as de Lacy was, but without the Irishman's joyous blackguardism. He was stupid looking, but underneath it he was a negotiator of great skilfulness, though what exactly he was negotiating O'Neill could not tell. He heard a lot of "His Grace," and "the Duke of Cornwall," and "when a certain person comes." But, beyond having a shrewd suspicion that there was treason against the Emperor in the air, he was utterly ignorant of what was toward. Sir Otho was cheek by jowl with the Master of the Temple; Sir Otho was friendly with the Patriarch; Sir Otho helped the poor Abyssinian Christians. Sir Otho's funds were boundless, it would seem.

"Who is this Duke?" O'Neill asked Josselyn once.

"I've only seen him once, Miles. He is a dour, scheming man."

"Where does he get all his money?"

"From the tin mines of Cornwall and the coal mines of Wales."

"And what does he want to be?"

"Emperor of Germany, I've heard."

"Too deep for me," O'Neill gave it up. So many people wanted to be so many things. Just now in Cyprus, Alice the Queen was claiming the throne of Jerusalem. She was the half-sister of King John de Brienne's wife. That made three claimants to the throne. Mentally it was very fatiguing. But so long as they were well horsed, cleanly fed, and regularly paid, O'Neill and Josselyn bothered not a whit about the intricacies of succession. Miles was glad that it was practically by force of the Temple de Lacy was made to quit the neighbourhood. The big man had ridden far and near looking for Miles' body, or for news of him; had wandered around the shores of the Dead Sea disguised as a Hospitaller friar. Only when he was satisfied there was nothing more to be done had he fled. The remains of the Irish troop he had sold to a German baron, giving them their back pay out of the proceeds. O'Neill was glad to hear how the big man had behaved. He was now with Queen Alice in Cyprus, of the body of knights urging her to attack Jaffa. Good old de Lacy! Miles wrote him in Cyprus, giving the letter to the care of an Armenian trader, but having little hope of its ever getting there. Even if it were delivered to him, Miles laughed to himself, he would think it some chandler's account or notary's instrument, and make the bearer eat it. And if the bearer told him that it was a letter from Sir Miles O'Neill, he would only consider it "a dirty native's trick," and send a servant for his whip. Ah, well, Miles would always have a corner in his heart warm for him.

Sir Otho, in the name of the mysterious "Duke," began a work of piety, which was really a police measure. Now that the Emperor and the Pope were at war, and that the Templars were busy with their campaign against the Sultan of Aleppo, there was none whose duty it was to keep a show of order in the Church of the Holy Sepulchre. Or rather there was none who had time or money to spend on it, and what with differences of nationality, and differences of rites, keeping order there was necessary. First, there were the European friars, following the ritual of Rome, shaven tonsured men, mostly Italian and French, with an occasional English monk. They kept to themselves, and tended the

Sepulchre and their altar on Calvary. The other sect gave them respect if not reverence, for behind them was the mailed hand of the Templars. Next came the Georgian sect, the traditional keepers of Calvary, small tonsured men, chattering in their mysterious tongue which was supposed to be Chaldean. The Greeks, with their pasty faces, their straggling beards and treacherous eyes, kept the Chauncel. Their warrant was from Constantine. The Syrians denied purgatory and kept four Lents in the year, and used Greek in their service. They were the aboriginal Christians. There were also *Goeti*, or Egyptian Christians, who kept the cave beneath Calvary, where they claimed Adam's skull was buried. They were timid, oppressed men. The Armenians kept the Pillar of Scourging, and looked down on all other Christian sects, because their Catholicos, they claimed, was the earthly representative of Saint Peter, who was first Bishop of Antioch. They fasted on Christmas Day, when the other sects were feasting. The Nestorians guarded the prison where Christ was kept and were mainly Mongols and Persians. There were also the Jacobites, some of whom were frail Indian men. Half-crazed with hunger and devotion the Maronites lay at the Church door. They had no rights in the Church, and nobody to feed them, and none to protect them.

Of all the sects in Saint Sepulchre the most curious and most mysterious of all were the Abyssinians. The church adjoining the Sepulchre's self was theirs. They were slight men, like gangling young girls, and black as night, except on the palms of their hands, which were pink. Their heads were shaven, and on each of their foreheads a cross was burned. Their frail necks and long African skulls gave them the appearance of strange exotic ghosts. Their copes were of gold, surpassing in richness the vestments of the Greeks. And none offered them injury. They were subjects of Prester John, whose letter to Emanuel, Prince of Constantinople, had produced amazement and fear and hope in the Christian and Saracen worlds. "Should you desire to learn the greatness and excellency of our Exaltedness and of the land subject to our sceptre," he had written to the Byzantine monarch, "then hear and believe: I, Presbyter Johannes, Priest by the Almighty Power of God and the Might of our Lord

Jesus Christ, King of Kings and Lord of Lords, surpass all under heaven in virtue, in riches, and in power; seventy-two kings pay us tribute. . . . In the three Indies our Magnificence rules, and our land extends beyond India, where rests the body of the holy apostle Thomas; it reaches toward the sunrise over the wastes, and it trends toward deserted Babylon near the tower of Babel. Seventy-two provinces, of which only a few are Christian, serve us. Each has its own king, but all are tributary to us.

"Our land is the home of elephants, dromedaries, camels, crocodiles, meta-collinarum, cametennus, tensevetes, wild asses, white and red lions, white bears, white merles, crickets, griffins, tigers, lamias, hyænas, wild horses, wild oxen and wild men, men with horns, one-eyed men, men with eyes before and behind, centaurs, fauns, satyrs, pygmies, forty-ell high giants, Cyclopses, and similar women; it is the home, too, of the phœnix, and of nearly all living animals. We have some people subject to us who feed on the flesh of men and of prematurely born animals, and who never fear death. When any of these people die, their friends and relations eat them ravenously, for they regard it as a main duty to munch human flesh. Their names are Gog and Magog, Anie, Agit, Azenach, Fomme-peri, Befari. . . . We lead them at our pleasure against our foes, and neither man nor beast is left undevoured, if our Majesty gives the requisite permission. When all our foes are eaten, then we return with our hosts home again. . . . "

One does not offer hurt or indignity to the subjects of an Emperor such as this. Both Maimonides and Benjamin of Tudela had confirmed the truth of his existence and state, and they, being Jews, were impartial. Nevertheless the people at Jerusalem found the Abyssinians to be a quiet-walking, quiet-spoken folk. But the natives at Jerusalem discovered even that to be sinister. They saw in the Middle Indians the quiet glossiness of deep fatal water.

Their services were like no other services in Saint Sepulchre. They stood in a ring wearing their golden copes, and they held little clappers of gold on their hands, and some had little bells of gold. They sang in high quavering voices and danced in a weird shuffling rhythm. Once O'Neill had

a layman of their cult translate their chanting into Arabic for his information. The
officiant stood in the middle of the circle
and piped in his thin aged voice:

"Before I am delivered up to them, let us
sing a hymn to the Father, and go forth to
what lieth before us.

"Glory to Thee, Father!"

And the circle sang:

"Glory to Thee, Word! Glory to Thee,
Grace! Amen.

"Glory to Thee, Spirit! Glory to Thee,
Holy One!

"Glory to the Glory. Amen."

"Now, whereas we give thanks, I say,"
the patriarch chanted:

"I would be saved, and I would save.
Amen.

"I would be loosed, and I would loose.
Amen.

"I would hear, and I would be heard.
Amen."

And then the circle would sing:

"I would be understood, being wholly
understanding. Amen."

"Grace is dancing," the old man would
pronounce.

The circle would begin shuffling.

"I would pipe. Dance all of you. Amen."

Under the dome of the vast church, the shuffling feet gave a sense of strange movement, as of the fated exact eternal stars. The golden clappers and the minuscule bells gave an eery ghost of music, like something one might hear from vast distances, as from a star.

"The Twelfth number is dancing above. Amen.

"And the Whole that can dance. Amen.

"He that danceth not, knoweth not what is being done. Amen."

And now O'Neill and the guard had to watch that no Byzantine fanatic with a knife drove through the dancing circle at the African prelate. If he did, all the Greek priests would disclaim the act, and suggest the man was a Frank. The Greeks came as close as they dared, and there was murder in their eyes. Their teeth showed, cruel as ferrets'. The English guards, with clumsy humour, drove them back with the butts of their pikes.

"I am a lamp to thee, who beholdest me. Amen.

"I am a mirror to thee who perceivest me. Amen.

"I am a door to thee who knockest at me. Amen.

"I am a way to thee, wayfarer. Amen."

The music of the golden clappers ceased. The dancing stopped. In the middle of the circle, what with the gloom of the great church, the old officiant's black head seemed to disappear, and the stiff golden cope seemed not to hold a body but a spirit. The aged voice became a whisper.

"Be ye also persuaded, therefore, beloved, that it is no man whom I preach unto you to worship, but God unchangeable, God invincible, God higher than all authority. . . . If ye then abide in him, and in him are builded up, ye shall possess your soul indestructible."

O'Neill translated as much of the service as he could remember for the benefit of Sir Otho's chaplain, Father John of Tewkesbury. He was a big-boned, white-haired man, a great favourite with the soldiers, and more deeply read in theology than was customary for a private chaplain.

"What do you make of it?" O'Neill asked him.

"There is enough heresy in it to burn the world with hell-fire," the chaplain told him.

"But your Reverence," Miles laughed, "has discovered foul heresies in the Eastern Christianities. Are we of the West then the only Orthodoxy?"

"The very only."

"What about this crowd of primitive Christians in France, the men with the white smocks?"

"Dangerous heresy."

"And in Scotland they're not so orthodox."

"No, unfortunately."

"And in Ireland."

"In Ireland they are most bloody pagans."

"And the Order of the Temp——"

"Hush, for God's sake. For the sake of God's Church, and our own poor lives, hush!"

O'Neill stopped his questioning. Father John of Tewkesbury's honest face had gone white as a winding sheet.

CHAPTER VI

I

O'NEILL often felt, as he stood in Saint Sepulchre, that he stood in a centre toward which converging rays of hatred focussed. And he thought where Christ's tomb is, is a curse. Armenian hates Roman, and Greek hates Copt, and all this priesthood sincere in their hatred and firm in their beliefs were only pawns in a game played by thin-blooded, clever men, cold in their padded ermine cloaks. Who was to have Constantinopolis, Frank or Greek? That was one of the games. And another game played by German and English was the opening of the great route through Hijr, Ἔγρι of the Greeks, the caravan route mentioned by Ptolemy and Pliny, by which gold and frankincense were brought from Happy Arabia. Past this, or this itself, was some short, forgotten road to the Indies and to wealth incalculable. The chivalry of high-minded knights, the stands of arms, the hysteric pilgrims, the ecstatic poets, the chanting priests, the very tomb of the Lord were only pawns in this vast game—whether Greek or Frank should have Constantine's city, or German or English control the perilous Indian highway. Very clearly now O'Neill saw it all. His brother-officer, young Josselyn, saw nothing of it. He only did his duty as he saw it. He came into Saint Sepulchre, knife in belt, heavy kurbash of camel hide in his right hand, with cheery words and a cold glint in his eye:

> " *Ou vintiesme an de mon aage,*
> " *Ou point qu' Amors prend le paage*
> " *Des jones gens, couchiez estoie*
> " *Une nuit, si com je souloie,*"

he would arrive singing the Romance of the Rose,

> " In my twentieth year of age,
> " When thoughts of love the budding
>   heart engage
> " One friendly night I lay asleep,
> " Cradled like some small vessel on
>   the deep. . . ."

And, "any trouble here?" his voice would ring out through the vaulted church. Oh, no, there was no trouble at all, they assured him. They spoke together, Latin, Georgian, and Greek, assuring his Knightliness that there had never been any, that it was all a grievous mistake. That his Knightliness was wasting his time was apparent. Surely there was no need of police, they cried indignantly, about God's grave. "Well, I'll just have a look round," Josselyn would say unmoved. The warring sects feared him. He was incorruptible, and had no doubts as to his duty. But O'Neill they feared even more. O'Neill, too, was incorruptible, but O'Neill was not stupid. He came in unarmed. He spoke to every sect. He listened to complaints with unwearying patience. They would give O'Neill small presents: the Greeks a sprig of the olive tree in which the horns of the ram were caught which Abraham sacrificed instead of Isaac his son; the Nestorians some minute thin coin of gold minted in India before Alexander's time; the Abyssinians some grotesque little carving out of Africa. To them all he was a friend, but just and terrible. They noticed it was

O'Neill commanded in the Sepulchre on the annual day when with bell and candles, with terrible cursing, the Greeks thundered the excommunication against Rome. On the visits of Sir Otho, rare enough God knows, to the Holy Sepulchre, the Irishman walked by his side as an equal. They saw all this.

But they did not see that with all his military knowledge, his growing fame, his breeding, his quick sense of men, he would have changed gladly with Josselyn; would have exchanged all for the Kentishman's joy in life and untroubled mind. The truth was O'Neill was weary of it. Even though he helped the shadowy Duke of Cornwall gain the promised highway to the Indies, yet what would he receive but some small barony of arid land, more than the Duke would give his favourite poet, less than he would give some gentlewoman for the surrender of her body. His heart was not turned to the Duke. If loyalty he had to any sovereign, it was to that shrivelled monkey-like blind man, whom he had never seen, and who never thought of him, beating his breast and making his soul in the Monastery of Donegal, Dark Hugh, the King of Ulster. A barony for Josselyn, a bit of land, and his unswerving English loyalty would satisfy the Kentish lad. If you were to ask him did he not want more, O'Neill thought, Josselyn would ask in wonder what more was there? Safe in tradition, safe in belief, safe in his small world, Josselyn was as in a well-defended tower, where he O'Neill felt naked and alone in the plain of the bare world.

The truth was that ever since he had come to Jerusalem, and especially since he had for duty the patrol of the Sepulchre, his quiet Irish faith in Christianity, as he had known it in Ireland, had been shaken to the core. He had not known it was so intricate a belief. The Greeks claimed that the Pope was not the successor of Peter but of Constantine the Emperor, who had never even been in Rome, and somehow it seemed they were right. The Roman clergy replied with arguments that seemed quite right too. The Abyssinians claimed that the Pope did not matter at all, seeing that Saint Peter didn't matter, Saint John being the only intimate and the only chronicler of the Lord. Both Greek and Roman turned on the Africans, snarling, and said their particular Gospel or Acts of John were a Gnostic forgery. Quietly in the other sects was preached an ecstatic doctrine that both Satan and Jesus were sons of God, one the elder and outcast, one the beloved. They pointed to the text: How thou art fallen from Heaven, Lucifer, thou Son of the morning. And after a period of religious frenzy of Christianity, it was whispered that they lapsed into dark rites. They loved the Lord and feared Lucifer, but who knew in the end whether Satan might not prevail? The inner circle of the Temple had thrown Christianity over, and when they spoke of the Impenitent Thief on the Cross, they meant Christ, who had stolen the Divinity of God. All in Jerusalem knew of their weird idol, Baphomet, Ancient of Days, whom by dark acts they made speak oracles; of their magic girdles worn under their habits; of their foul secret ritual. None dared speak out. None knew when the dark dagger of the Temple would strike, darker and surer than the knives of the sicarii of the Jewish patriots, than the hooked knives of the mad zealots who owned the Old Man of the Mountain as chief. Of all the sects in Jerusalem, O'Neill's sympathy was with the occasional Jewish pilgrims, who, at peril of their lives, and by courtesy of the Temple, and with a great price purchased the right to kiss the walls of Solomon's edifice, and to say their litany. Rich bankers of Frankfort, polished thinkers of Lisbon, advisers to Italian princes, they rocked to and fro and wept, and whispered their tragic prayer:

"On account of the Palace which is laid
    wasted,
"We sit solitary, and weep.
"For the sake of the Temple, which is
    destroyed,
"We sit solitary, and weep.
"For the walls that are thrown down,
"We sit solitary, and weep.
"For our glory, which hath departed from
    us,
"We sit solitary, and weep.
"For our wise men, who have perished,
"We sit solitary, and weep.
"For the precious stones, which are
    burnt,
"We sit solitary, and weep.
"For our priests, which have fallen,
"We sit solitary, and weep . . .
"May peace and happiness enter Zion,
"May the Rod of Power turn towards
    Jerusalem!"

Among these folk, however you felt about them, there were no difficulties of belief, no schisms, and when they kissed the courses of great stone laid by Solomon, they were kissing something definite and historically known to be true. But, and here was the thing O'Neill could not stomach, the Holy Sepulchre, learned men said, was not the Holy Sepulchre at all. It could not have been it. It was within the known walls of Jerusalem, and therefore was out of court. The sainted Queen Helena, who had started as a dancing girl and ended as a nun, had just pitched on that as a likely place, and claimed to have discovered the Holy Cross in it. The true site was down past the Temple in the little fields toward Jordan.

And, O'Neill thought, they had spilled a thousand tuns of chivalrous blood for a graveyard in which after all He was never buried. Oh, Body of God! What a mad, damned, and bloody world!

II

His thoughts now were always homing to Damascus, as birds home. In fetid Jerusalem, always, it would seem, short of water, he thought of cool Damascus, where the fertile rill the Greeks called the Golden River ran through street and house and garden. It had a little song, that river, the Barada, impossible to put to music or to words, but it was like an accompaniment to the growing of the peach trees and the blossoming almond. And there was ever drowsy white-headed Hermon nodding in the distance. The Moorish gardeners, the growers of fruit, tended golden orange and green fig with a celestial gravity in their faces, for was this not Adam's business? In the bazaars the white- and round-faced merchants sat, quiet as players of chess. They were not out to make outrageous profits, for this was forbidden by their volume of sacred law, but to play a game as skilful as chess, and they hated nothing more than a man who knew what he wanted, and how much he wanted to pay for it; that gave no play to their curious subtle minds. And in the bazaars and quiet squares went the real Arab, the great-limbed, calm-eyed bronze men whose wealth was in flocks, in curious woven carpets, in great strings of amber, in weapons inlaid with gold; the men who followed the patriarchal tradition of Abraham, *Khalil Ullah*, The Friend of God. Calm-eyed, sure of their destiny, the sheykhs ruled the moon-faced Damascenes and black Moroccan gardeners, with warm hearts and iron hands. By God! O'Neill thought, they were men, those! Convinced of the truth of their revelation, they had ventured everything on it, fighting their way into China of the East, into Africa, into Spain, to Vienna's walls. Their sea-captains had raided Cornwall and Devonshire, and the shores of Bantry Bay in his own country, and had sailed truculently up to Galway pier. By God! but they got their bellyful of fighting on the dressed blocks of Connemara. . . . They discovered they weren't the only people who had a humour of war. Great fighters, gallant victors, in defeat noble—these Arabs. In a word, O'Neill decided, they were men.

From what he knew of their religion, it was a man's creed. There was but one God, they cried. . . . Theirs was no pantheon of old paganism, or trinity of modern subtleties. God was God! that was all. Mohammad was the messenger of God! Their mosques were miracles of space and coolness and quiet beauty. They had no doubts as to who was Father, and what was the exact position of the Son. Nor did they ever flirt with the powers of darkness, as did the Eastern Christians. To them Lucifer was "Satan, who was stoned." From the beautiful Minaret of the Bride in Damascus, the muazzin would proclaim in his voice that throbbed like a bell, that God was greatest, that God was One, and the Lord Mohammad was the Sent One of God. The great fountain, where one must cleanse himself before prayer, flashed in the court of the Mosque. In its cool enclosure there were no secret prayers, or intricacy of ritual, no reek of incense and sweat and foul clothing, as there were in Saint Sepulchre. There was not even a priest. The imam who explained the Koran was a man speaking to men.

O'Neill would see the simple pageantry of Arab life in Damascus, the mother of cities. He would see their simple creed. Feel their simple hearts. It was like looking into that crystal ball the Venetian soothsayers showed you You saw it all clearly *in petto*. And then, as in the magic glass, the scene clouded milkily, and clearing again, alive in his heart and his eyes, was the vision of the Arab lady, the sister of Ali, whose profile was like the Greek heads Venetian merchants traded in from Athens, whose lithe body you sensed would have given Phidias, that antique sculptor of the Greeks, a model for Spirit clothed in the April of beauty.

III

He had thought in the first week of his captivity when he saw her in sheykhly dress, going to and fro, aping the man, that here was a creature vain, spoiled and arrogant. He naturally distrusted her, with his Irish mistrust of all women. He invented an alternative explanation, that was even more displeasing. There were tales of tribes in the North where the men fought and afterwards the women mutilated the fallen enemies. She might be one of those, he thought, not yet developed, but in training for the part. Only later he began to see that there was some quirk in the old sheykh Haroun's head, perhaps an occult hurt from the mace of Lionheart, which made the old chieftain regard her as his son. The old man had loved the mother of Ali and Kothra, with the intense love many of the Arab know, and when she died, his love had gone into the children. At the age of ten Ali had died, and now Kothra was the only living reminder of the emotional epic of the chieftain's heart. As an Arab he wanted a son. He had a daughter who would ride with him, who strove to take the son's place, so that at times he could imagine the beloved Ali was there. She was an independent girl, a girl of the desert, not a woman of the Syrian towns. A girl who knew sunrise and starlight, had the Bedouin love for a horse, and an ancient Greek disdain of small events. He had not ever thought of her as a woman until once he hobbled into the garden of Sheykh Haroun's Damascus house, and saw her in woman's dress, with a rose in her hand, talking to the Moorish gardener.

She wore the long white garments of a Syrian lady. Small slippers of gold brocade flashed on her feet. She wore the white closely fitting cap of Egyptian linen coming down to her eyebrows of gold. But instead of the dreadful grave-like veil of Syria, she had thrown loosely about throat and mouth a scarf of heavy silk broidered with gold. O'Neill turned to hobble away again.

"Come into the sun, Sheykh O'Neill," she called clearly. "Do not be anxious. This is no Egyptian harem. This is a man's house." And coming forward she laid her firm white hand on his arm. "Sit here a while in the sun," she said. There was a marble seat by the little stream in the garden. "Not that way," she forced him round. "Keep your back to the sun, and your head in the shade of the tree." She took his sticks from him, when he had lowered himself to the seat. "Is all well with you in my father's house?"

"I am very comfortable," he said, "and very grateful."

"You must not be grateful, Sheykh O'Neill. You are the guest of the Bani Iskander. When sheykhs meet, there is no talk of gratitude surely." A shrill whistle in the tree startled O'Neill, and looking up he saw a lemur with beautiful silver fur and face of a negro dwarf looking at him with overwise eyes. "Oh Father of Naughtiness!" she chided it. "It is a friend of mine, Sheykh

O'Neill," she explained, "it possesses a mixture of childishness and old man's cunning such as you could hardly believe. And there are two other friends of mine." She gave a clear high call, and a small Syrian bear with a beautiful silver mask of fur, and a splendid hound came down the path. "This is the Simple One," she introduced the bear, not much larger than a lamb, "I bought him from a *sany*, a travelling desert smith. They capture them in the Lebanon when cubs, and bring them into es-Sham in small leathern bags. He is a nuisance. Art thou not a nuisance, O Inventor of Iniquity?" she bent down and pulled it to its haunches. There was a clumsy and appealing look about the little animal that made one laugh. "He climbs trees for oranges, so that I have disputes with Ali Hassan, the head gardener, about him, most grim disputes. And he has a drunkard's passion for honey, so that we may keep no bees. And this one," she turned to the hound, "is named the Father of Swiftness. He was given me by a cousin now dead, who got him where the mountains of Crim Tartary join the Indian lands." The gazelle hound was beautiful, with its lovely coat and noble face. It had the face of a nobleman. "He is of very ancient lineage, Sheykh O'Neill. The Tartars keep the pedigree of these dogs, as we Arabs cherish the pedigree of our horses." The bear began boxing clumsily at the fine hound, but the dog moved gently aside. The girl tossed the rose to the honey-bear. He caught it deftly in his futile-looking paws and began eating it. She looked for a long minute at O'Neill.

"Why do you fight, Sheykh O'Neill?" she asked.

"I do not understand you."

"Some fight for money, and some for fame, and some for a cause they know to be true. For which reason do you wage war?"

"I suppose there was nothing else for me to do. I had no other resources."

"Then you are a hired soldier." There was surprise in her voice.

O'Neill flushed. "I had never thought of it in that way before, but I am afraid you are right. I am a hired soldier."

There was a faint line between her eyebrows, a note of wonder. "And yet," she said, "I should have taken you to be of princely blood."

"Of as princely," O'Neill said proudly, "as runs in any king's veins." He looked around the garden; he looked at the dog and bear; he looked at herself shining in rich Syrian silks and gold. "I suppose it has never occurred to you that there is such a thing as being poor. It's rather a horrible thing."

"Is it?" she said. "My father's brother, Sheykh Ibrahim, renounced all his possessions to be a dervish in the College at Cairo. He owns nothing but his dervish dress. He eats nothing but black bread and water, and those, according to his vow, he must beg, and yet he has a noble, happy face. To him poverty is a blessing."

The old physician came into the garden. He saw Kothra, and noted O'Neill's flushed face, and downcast head.

"Ho, thou who art witless," he told the girl, "what have you done to my ill one?" He passed his hand over O'Neill's brow. "You are no woman, sister of Ali, but a waspish boy." The girl looked as if she were going to cry.

"She said nothing to me but truths," O'Neill interrupted.

"Is mutton food for a sucking child? Or truths for a sick man?" the physician grumbled. "I never held with this mumming. Women are women and men are men, by God! Put a leopard skin on a goat, and he thinks: Ho, where is mine enemy the lion?"

O'Neill smiled, and suddenly through her tears the girl smiled too. "Consider the mule!" rambled on the hakeem.

"I am a woman," Kothra flared up, "I am a woman, friend of my father, and you yourself have said, a very beautiful one."

"Ho, thou who art vain!" snorted the old physician.

Their kindness to him during his convalescence was embarrassing. Kothra sent to Jerusalem for wine of Oporto, the full-blooded Portuguese wine to help him to health, and her Moorish slaves were for ever doing something for him. The wine seemed such a kind thought, and he was put about to drink it in a Moslem house, but Kothra and the physician stood by him. Still out of courtesy he refused. "Wallah! he will always think I am going to poison him, this one!" Kothra said impatiently, and seizing the glass drank a mouthful. She choked and spluttered, and ran out of the garden.

"See what you have done, boy, with your obstinacy," the physician said. "You have made a Moslem woman drink wine."

"She has sinned in her creed," O'Neill said aghast.

"She has not sinned," said the old physician. "Sin is in the intention. Drink your wine, boy, and get well."

They told him news of Jerusalem, of how the Emperor Frederick was on the point of concluding a truce with the sultans of Egypt and Syria, and how the Pope had directed that no priest in Jerusalem was to officiate at his coronation were he to come there. No loyalty was to be shown him, and all in Jerusalem had agreed to do the Pope's behest, save only the Templars, who had refused to side with either Pope or Emperor. Of de Lacy they had no news, and O'Neill could see that they despised the Irish captain. One evening, in the quiet Damascene dusk, he told Sheykh Haroun and the old physician, and Kothra, and the cousins Mohammad and Abdallah, the story of his life. They sat in a circle around the brass brazier of glowing charcoal, and shook their heads, and uttered many oaths.

"But the sheykh of Ulster," Abdallah said. "I cannot understand him. To sit quietly and pray while the son of his brother's son is being wronged. Wallah! that is not the way of the Arab."

"Old men are selfish," Sheykh Haroun nodded. "They hate to be bothered. Who knows the selfishness of old men better than I, who am both selfish and old?"

"No! No! Uncle Haroun. No! No! Father of Ali!" they all cried. "There is none greater-hearted than you."

But the old man shook his head. "Only God knoweth!" he said. "God and I." And he tapped the brazier with his sheykh's wand.

"But Sheykh O'Neill," Mohammad leaned forward, "why do you hold and fight with the Frankish knights who dispossessed you? Cannot you see, they are your enemies, O'Neill?"

"You cannot turn against a whole race for what one family has done, Mohammad, and besides, one must have loyalties."

"Wallah! the lad is right," the old sheykh cried. "For if a man have no loyalties, what can he have but profits? And though profits can ease the road of the body for a little space, they can never ease the road of the mind. And you are right, Sheykh O'Neill, in being true to your captain, pirate though he be."

"I knew," Kothra said quietly, "that you were not a hired soldier."

"But I am a hired soldier," O'Neill laughed, " else what am I?"

"You are one who has come along a road in darkness, O'Neill, and are waiting for the light. And when the light comes, you will see your course of pilgrimage. We of the Arab," she looked into the fire, " are hoping that the light may come to you in Damascus." She paused. O'Neill said nothing.

She turned around to him, suddenly, and looked straight at him. "O'Neill, has a light come?" she asked.

Miles had a sense that the old sheykh and Mohammad and Abdallah, and the hakeem's self, were waiting intently for his answer.

"No," he said firmly, "no, sister of Ali. No light has come."

"I will not have my sick one bothered," said the physician bluffly, "by talk of This and talk of That. Ho! to thy bed, thou!" he put his arm around O'Neill's shoulders, "with thy broken bones!"

With the coming of Sheykh Ibrahim, O'Neill got an inkling into Arab belief which astounded him. The dervish was older than his brother Haroun. He wore a close-fitting turban of green, a linen jacket and wide, pleated linen skirt. Sandals were on his brown feet. One got somehow the impression of an aged rain-washed tree. There was a feeling of kindness about him, but an aloof, impersonal kindness, like sunshine. One felt he had been long away from the world. With him were three young dervishes, who had an ascetic, fanatic look. From the disciples O'Neill learned that Sheykh Ibrahim was the *Qutb*, the most eminent saint of the time.

He went with Sheykh Haroun to the great mosque to hear the mystic speak. He had thought it impossible for any Christians to enter a Moslem place of prayer, but the Arabs had smiled. "So long as he come as a friend . . . ." Haroun had replied. In the court-yard, in the moonlight which threw strange shadows, Ibrahim and his pupils were dancing. Three flutes and a small throbbing drum gave the music, and as the men span around, their white linen skirts standing out like ruffs, their balloon-like drawers wrapped around their muscular legs with the swiftness of spinning. Their hands were held on high, and on each of their faces was the print of ecstasy. The thin wail of the flutes and the disturbing throb of the drum, and the ghostly figures dancing in the moonlight while the mosque was crowded with silent figures, gave O'Neill a sense akin to fright. There was something so unearthly in it all. The sailing moon overhead was like a friendly village to him compared to the weird silence of the vast mosque. Then the flutes and the drum and the dancing ceased.

O'Neill felt the Damascenes against the wall lean forward, surge forward sitting, as a wave curls before it breaks. The *Qutb* was going to speak. He stood up in the moonlight, a tall thin brown man. Behind him were his disciples. One was a Persian, with a delicate girl's face. One was a squat Tartar, with high cheek-bones and almond eyes. One was a gigantic Saharan negro.

The old man's bell-like voice went through the mosque.

"Jesus passed three men," he said slowly. "Their faces were white as snow and their bodies lean as a knife. He questioned them: 'Ho! Ye that are haggard, what hath brought you to this plight?' They spoke: 'Fear of the Flames.' Jesus said: 'You dread a thing created, and it behoves God that he should save those who fear.' Jesus passed three others. Their faces were white as the bleached bones of camels, and their flesh hung on their frames. He questioned them: 'Ho! Ye who are lean, what hath brought you to this state?' They spoke: 'Longing for Paradise.' Jesus said: 'Ye desire a thing created, and it behoves God that He should grant you what you suffer for.'

"Jesus passed three men. Their faces were like mirrors of light, their bodies were frail as blossoms. Jesus questioned them: 'Ho! Ye who are like petals in the wind, what hath brought you to this?' They spoke: 'Our love of God.' Jesus said: 'Ye are the nearest to Him, ye are the nearest to Him.'"

The sheykh and three disciples turned

suddenly and walked out of the mosque. Kothra's cool hand caught O'Neill's wrist.

"Ho! Father of Ali! Abdallah, Mohammad, close about lest our guest be hurt in this crowd."

"I don't understand." O'Neill was bothered.

"You don't understand what?" the sister of Ali caught his undertone.

"He spoke of Jesus."

"Ho! then! Do the Nassara think they own Jesus, as a merchant owns his bags of corn, with now a little to be sold, a little to be given away! See there," she pointed to the wall of the mosque, and faintly gleaming in the moonlight O'Neill could discern faint Byzantine letters in gold. "When, in the decadence of Christianity, this ancient place was taken by the men of Islam, and all material created things, all statues made in the likeness of men and women broken and shattered, those letters were allowed to remain. I cannot read the Greek, but I know what they mean. They say: Thy Kingdom, O Christ, is an enduring Kingdom."

"And those were not chiselled out?"

"Why should they be?" the sister of Ali said. "Are they not true?"

IV

In the heat and sweat and grime, in the suspicion and the terror of Jerusalem, the memory of Damascus would come to him, like a story he had heard, like a story the wandering Arab tale-tellers spoke to their gaping audience outside the Golden Gate, from the epic of Queen Sharazad: some tale of a kalendar who had wandered into an enchanted house, or of a merchant of Bassorah, who had left his silks and pearls and frankincense to walk in the quiet of the town, and, opening a door ajar, had found himself in the garden of some king's enchanted daughter. The shallow river that trilled over the small polished stones; the kindly trees, with their rich varnished leaves; the clumsy honey bear going about on its hind legs as though it were a child learning to walk; the mischievous lemur whistling and chattering, the great dignified Afghani hound, sitting or standing always a picture of beauty and strength. Sometimes the wind would blow eastward from the Lebanon, and there would be the little chill of distant snow in the air, and the great hound would rise uneasily. He would be troubled by a dim memory of homeland, and O'Neill would say: "Poor old boy!" Kothra would throw him a quick look.

She loved sitting in the garden, doing her beautiful embroidery with gold thread on Damascus silk. All the work of gold on her garments was done by herself. O'Neill was amazed to know that the entire house was directed by her with one old Moorish slave as her aid. She was always an amazement. Sometimes when he came out into the garden he would find her singing, the clear shaking Arab notes having a sense of resting in the air like a shower of gold, or a lovely laburnum tree in the cool green garden. Sometimes she would stop singing, and nothing would persuade her to go on. And at other times she would begin singing in his presence, and go on with it, as though her heart and bosom were full and she must empty them. So that the wayfarers without the garden walls would stop to hear her, and gather in number, and at the end of each verse would cry: "Allah! Allah! Allah! Allah!" in enthusiasm, until at last some gust of shame would come over her, and she

would run down the garden, muffling her
face, laughing nervously.

> "Elijah hath a chariot," she once sang,
> "Of gold and flame.
> "Elisha sails a galley
> "Of enduring fame.
> "David's son, King Solomon,
> "Hath all magic arts.
> "But the little Lord Jesus
> "Owneth our hearts."

O'Neill looked at her keenly. She smiled
and went on,

> "Moses hath authority
> "From Sinai's rocks.
> "Abraham hath a myriad
> "Of silver flocks.
> "David hath all treasure,
> "Garnered in wars.
> "But the little Lord Jesus
> "Is crowned with stars."

"That is a Christian's song, sister of Ali,"
he told her. She shook her head.

> "Our Lord Mohammad
> "Stands at God's right.
> "Moses, the prophet,
> "Shines with God's light.

CRUSADE

"Gabriel, the Angel,
"Acts as God deems.
"But by the green hills of Heaven
"The Lord Jesus dreams."

"Captain Lord Mohammad,
"Rides from world to world;
"His bright sword in his right hand,
"His green flag unfurled.
"Bearded Admiral Noe
"Sails to starry deeps.
"But after long anguish,
"The Lord Jesus sleeps."

"What is that song, Kothra?" he asked.
"It is a song of the Syrian women, Sheykh
O'Neill, in the days when the autumn is
done, and the corn garnered, and the men
home from the seas, or from voyages to
Egypt or the Tartar lands. The little breath
of winter comes over the land, and into the
heart of everyone, like a gentle memory of
death. The men of Islam speak and sing
more of Abraham, the friend of God, but
they love the gentle prophet, the greatest
earth can ever see. But the Arab men
speak little of what they love. That is why
they never speak of their women, and you
of the setting sun think that to them on

this account women are cattle. But women are brave in their loves, O'Neill. They speak out. That is a song of the Syrian women. Also it is a charm against devils, and against serpents and wolves."

"But is that our Jesus?"

"No," she turned on him savagely. "It is not your Jesus. Everything is not yours: the land of the Arab, the wealth and citadels of the Arab, and the Asa ibn-Mariam of the Arab. It is the Jesus of all the world."

"But Jesus was murdered at Jerusalem."

"Jesus never died. A seeming of Jesus died on the gallows. Mohammad died. Noah died. Abraham died. Moses died. But Jesus never died. He was born of the Spirit of God. Not the soft breath of April was more gentle than he. Is not God the Compassionate, the Compassionating?"

"No, Kothra. It's proven."

"Out of books. O Lord of all the world! Can the trick of writing with a pen make a man infallible? And listen to this, O'Neill. The real books are dead. My uncle, Sheykh Ibrahim the dervish, will prove to you that. He will prove it to you out of the books themselves. There is no book my uncle Sheykh Ibrahim has not read. He could also write great books, O'Neill. But he teaches from his mind to the other minds. And if he wrote it down, what interpretation he puts on words might not be understood by those who read, so that he first teaches his disciples. Even the wicked one, the Sheykh el-Djebal, the Old Man of the Mountains, as you call him, who is cynic in all things, gives my uncle his due of reverence."

But the faith of the chief of the dervishes was too subtle for O'Neill. Kothra led him to where the saint was sitting quietly with his three pupils. The brown-faced man looked at them with eyes that seemed fixed on the end of the world.

"O father's brother!" she said O'Neill could see that the disciples were displeased at their intrusion; "will you tell the Nasarene knight that Jesus did not die?"

"Since he did not receive his life from the Angel of Death, how could he give it up to him?"

"But, father's brother," the sister of Ali said impatiently, "that is of all of us. Listen, what I have been saying is this: That Allah is so compassionate that he would not permit Jesus to die on the gallows tree."

"The compassion of Allah is beyond counting," the dervish said slowly. "It is reported of Abu 'l-Hasan Kurqani that one night of his praying he heard a Voice: 'Ho, Abu 'l-Hasan. Dost thou wish Me to tell the populace what I know of thee, that they may stone thee to death?' 'O Lord of all the worlds,' Abu 'l-Hasan said, 'dost Thou wish me to tell the people what I know of Thy Mercy and what I perceive of Thy Grace, that none of them may ever again bow to Thee in prayer?' The Voice answered: 'Keep thy secret, Abu 'l-Hasan, and I will keep Mine.'"

"O Sheykh Ibrahim," she looked ashamed and perturbed, "will you tell our friend, and explain it to him that his religion is wrong and ours is right?"

The Persian disciple nodded into a sort of trance like a flower nodding. What was behind the Tartar's orange mask none could say. But the giant black man from the Sahara seemed impatient. The *Qutb* picked a handful of sand from the path and let it run through his fingers.

"Faith is capable of every form," he said slowly. "It is a pasture for gazelles and a convent for Christian monks.

"And a temple for idols, and the pilgrim's Kaba, and the tables of the Torah, and the book of the Koran.

"It will follow the way of God, whichever road His camels take."

The Saharan dervish came toward Kothra and O'Neill. "You must go now," he said, and led them away. "Listen. What the chief dervish says is not for you. Simple things such as you want to know, I shall tell you. There are two things in Islam, Truth and the Law. The Truth is that God is One, and the Law is the Koran. It is written in the Koran that Asa ibn-Mariam was from the Spirit of Allah. Can anything of the spirit of Allah die and the world not founder? No! Then all is proven to you. Children, go in peace."

She seemed hurt and disappointed as they walked down the almond alley to the fountain where the small Chinese fish, red and gold, swam in a basin of rose red marble, fed by Barada, the golden river. She looked as if she were on the point of crying.

"Sister of Ali," O'Neill said softly to comfort her, "I like your simple faith better than all the wisdom of your uncle, and all the dogma of the Cairene dervish."

She turned and faced him. He could see between the muffling scarf and the close-fitting Moslem cap, that her grey eyes were filled with tears. "There," he put his hand into the folds of his coat and pulled out a handkerchief of linen, "sister of Ali, wipe your eyes. Don't be such a child."

She dabbed at them quickly as though ashamed of herself.

"O'Neill," she said, "if I do something for you, will you understand that it is because you are a friend, and you have been kind to me, and not for any other reason?"

"Of course, small hostess, I shall understand," he smiled.

"No, but you don't know what it is," she said. All the assumed mannishness, all the grave womanhood had dropped from her; and she seemed very much like a child one humours. O'Neill could now understand the vast love with which her people enveloped her. This was not the young sheykh who rode in the Arab raids or the capable mistress of slaves, but a small secret flower that had blossomed as a miracle in the Arab soil. "Please you will not misunderstand?"

"I don't know what it is, Kothra," he said—it was the first time he had used the little name, and he had done it unwittingly, but with its slender consonants it sounded like some softly-breathed bar of music. "Whatever it is, I shall not misunderstand."

"Folk who are friends are close to one another, and know one another. Where masks exist, you speak to a thing of fancy, not to a person you know. Friends must know each other. You have told us the story of your youth, and each day we see you. You know my father and my uncle, and my cousins, and how I manage our house, and why I ride with my father to round-ups of cattle and on the battle-raids, to give him the sense that the son he lost is riding by his saddle-flaps, the son whom he would never replace. You know this, O'Neill, and you know my pets to whom I talk, the clumsy honey-bear, the Tartar hound, and the lemur who thieves like some urchin of the gutter."

"You have been so utterly kind, Kothra, you have shown me everything."

"No," she said, "I have not shown you this."

So deftly, so quickly did she do it, that he hardly followed the gesture by which the scarf came from about throat and chin and mouth, and the white Arab cap came from her head. "*A Ree an Dhone!*" he said in Irish. "O King of the World."

He had seen something like it before, a beautiful Greek woman's head in stone, brought to Jerusalem by a Venetian lord from Athens, who said he could never marry after seeing that miracle of marble. It was said that Great Frederick had offered the noble of Venice half Sicily for the sculpture but he would not part with it. And now O'Neill saw a more perfect face and head, not in marble but in life. The gold of her eyebrows had only given a hint of the mass of wavy, close-bound gold that was her hair, gold so fined that it was all but silver, that had been concealed by the head-dress. From the border of the tied silken shirt, the neck rose in a graceful column like music. The small chin was like ivory turned by a craftsman's lathe, and the firm mouth had the tint of strawberries. Above the nose that would have baffled the fingers of Phidias, the brave grey eyes looked at him with a half-fear in them. He remembered where he had seen their tint before. It was in the deep clear waters of Galilee before the sun came to noontime. Her brow was not less white, not less smooth than the soft linen which had covered it a moment before.

"Yes, that is Kothra," she said.

He turned aside, such a swift surge had come into his heart. In all the words he knew it was hard to choose. When he looked at her again the cap was over her head, the scarf was about throat and chin and mouth.

He said: "There are things one expects from men, from a brotherhood of arms, from affection, from folk whose selves and whose forbears have been reared to know that nothing is good but honour. But I did not expect a gesture Homer should have written from a woman." He paused. "Sister of Ali, I don't say much, but a part of my young days was spoiled by a mother who was sour as spoiled wine, and the women who love to hear of spilled blood while they lie in their bowers disgust me, and the women of the seaports with their wet mouths . . .

their mouths are the gateways of hell. I am clumsy with my words. It is as if a girl of four laid her rose-leaf fingers on my battered hands, and I was filled with pity that anything so innocent must go through the desperate battle that life is. Her fingers are not laid on your hands but are grasping the artery of your heart. Also, Kothra, never will I be out in the half light, looking out for the evening star to show, but with its appearing I shall see your face. And when, in the sweat and shouting and the hacking of battle, my moment of ending will come, as I know it must, the last thing I shall see before the darkness closes is—what you have shown me." He laughed. "It's a ridiculous thing to utter, but in all the stupid clutter of words I know, I can only find: thank you."

"O'Neill," she said very softly, "I knew you would not misunderstand."

V

The one thing the cousins Mohammad and Abdallah could never explain to each other was how O'Neill had killed the turcoman captain with his hands alone. The Tartar leader had not been a favourite with the Bani Iskander. Though he had professed Islam yet there had always been doubts as to his sincerity, and it was rumoured that he still owned queer Tibetan idols to whom he made sacrifices. He had been a wine-bibber. Also he was a mercenary soldier. Abdallah and Mohammad and many of the leaders had discussed his death, and had decided that there must have been some weakness in him to have dropped so easily. "Is it not so, O'Neill?"

"No, Sheykh Mohammad," O'Neill said. "It was an intended blow." And he explained how the warlike Irish tribes, disarmed after their defeat by the Danes, had evolved a manner of fighting as deadly as with weapons. It was a servant's fighting, but O'Neill happened to know it. They brought him a great Stambuly wrestler, a giant of a man, quivering with flesh. "Can you show Abdallah how it is done?" they asked.

They were in the garden at dusk. Kothra, in her sheykh's clothes, sat by her father. The chief of the dervishes with his three disciples sat and looked on, aloof, with eyes that saw only with the surface, their minds being on some problem of Koranic philosophy. Abdallah and Mohammad, big muscular men, whose only interests were flocks and horses and fighting, looked at O'Neill. The Stambuly wrestler stood vast and deferential in this assembly of sheykhs. He had flung off his clothes, and stood in leathern loin-cloth, bare-footed, with all his Turk's white bulk. Abdallah wore only his baggy Syrian drawers from waist to ankle. His brown torso was like a figure of the Greeks cast in a mould of bronze.

"Can he be thrown, O'Neill?" The Turkish professional shook his head. His battered mouth was in a shrewd grin.

"Easily," Miles said. He rose up, his left arm in its sling. "No! No!" Abdallah protested. "Just show me and I'll do it."

"It's all right, Abdallah. I shan't be hurt," O'Neill went forward smiling toward the lumbering man. The Turk seemed to squat, like a toad. He watched O'Neill out of small toad's eyes. O'Neill smiled at him. The wrestler's head drew into his shoulders, like a turtle's head retiring into his shell.

O'Neill moved to the right. The wrestler moved in time with him shuffling his feet. The man began to have a look of doubt and stupidity in his eyes. His vast arms, like men's legs, were poised. His hands hooked. O'Neill laughed.

Then, like the quick dart of a snake, O'Neill's right hand caught the wrestler's right wrist. O'Neill's right foot locked around the wrestler's right ankle. A quick tug and the naked Turk pitched forward on his face. He slid on his face on the ground like some weird, uncomely monster fish, flung out of a net on to dry ground.

"Wallah!" the cousins swore in astonishment. Sheykh Haroun nodded his head vigorously. The old dervish smiled faintly around the corners of his eyes. The Persian disciple drooped more beautifully than ever. The Tartar grinned openly. Only the Saharan dervish looked severe and bored, as though these things were vulgarities hard to be borne. And then suddenly the Turk on the ground did the strangest thing. He began to cry.

"You see, O'Neill," Abdallah said, "he has never been thrown before."

"Tell him, Abdallah, it is not real wrestling. It is only a trick."

"Fo! it is nothing," the sister of Ali said contemptuously. "My uncle Ibrahim when young could make all the tables in the room swim in the air. Is it not so, Uncle Ibrahim?" she said to the dervish.

"Seeing that the lifting of the cup to the lips by the hand," the old dervish spoke, "is not the action of the hand, but the action of the brain and will, beloved, it must be true in principle that the cup can be lifted without even the hand. When I was young I did these things to prove the principle true. But now, I have found that the brain and will are only instruments, and I have nothing to do with instruments. There is only the soul praying that is good. Oh, little Kothra, were a real saint to pray every fish in the sea would stop swimming lest the faint beating of its fins should disturb the communion with God."

"But Uncle Ibrahim, you can calm madness, and stop the murderer's knife in mid-air."

"These things are vouchsafed me, but what Sheykh O'Neill has done is a learnt thing. It is of Archimedes, the Greek."

O'Neill and Abdallah calmed the crying athlete, Abdallah giving him presents, and Miles proceeded to teach the Arab various locks of wrist and head, and how a blow with the edge of the hand is more effective than seven blows with the clenched fist. Suddenly the big Arab threw his naked arm around O'Neill's neck.

"O beloved," he said, "will you stay with the Arab, who are your lovers and friends?"

"I can't, Abdallah."

"Listen, O'Neill, I am no merchant. I offer you nothing. Also, I tell you a secret thing. The Khorasanic barbarians under their Aga, Barbarquan, are planning to over-run Syria with fire and sword, and we need great-hearted fighting men. Stay with us, dear one, and be a chief of the Bani Iskander. Only say: there is no God but God, and the Lord Mohammad is the Sent One of God."

"I know, Abdallah," O'Neill shook his head. "If I could I would."

"Just the one short phrase, O'Neill. There is no God but God, and Mohammad is the messenger of God."

"I think I can say: there is no God but God. And as to the Lord Mohammad——" he paused.

"The Sent One of God," urged Abdallah.

"I believe him to have been a great man. I believe that none but a great and good man could have influenced friends, and country, and the Eastern world as he has done. To have stamped out idols, abolished drunkenness, killed usury, established fellowship are the acts of a man of God. Yes, I believe him to have been the Messenger of God."

"Ho, Moslems in the East and Moslems in the West," the brazen throat of Abdallah rang in the dusk, "welcome a brother in Islam!"

"No, Abdallah!" O'Neill was firm. "I do not accept Islam."

"But you said," the big man looked at him heavily, "but you said that God is One, and you believed the Lord Mohammad to be the Messenger of God!"

The old dervish stood up. With a motion of his little finger he called his disciples. They stood up like statues in their pleated skirts, their little jackets, their tall caps of green felt. Their bare feet seemed hardly to touch the ground. They were like players of the Magi in some Christian pomp of God's nativity, the beautiful drooping Persian boy, the masked Tartar, whose face was a mask, the giant negro. "Ho! Ye who are stupid," the chief of the dervishes cried, "when will ye know the simplest thing, as that believing and believing-to-be are as strangers who pass in the dark!" He came over and put his hands on O'Neill's shoulders. "Hearken thou who art young. The Old Wandering Beggar will tell you a secret." He kissed O'Neill on both cheeks. "You must never forget this: God is a friend."

He turned abruptly and walked down the garden. The disciples seemed to float after him. Their white garments were like silver pillars in the dusk, and then they were gone.

"I suppose they are gone to the mosque," O'Neill said. He wanted to say something, to break the strange discomforting silence.

"They are gone," Kothra said, " none knows whither. To Khorassan perhaps, or to Persia, or westward to the Land of the Moors."

"But they did not say good-bye."

"They never say good-bye."

"Where are their camels picketed?"

"They have no camels."

"But who will carry their food and water-skins?"

"They have no food or waterskins," Kothra answered.

"And is nobody to guide or feed them in the bleak desert lands?" O'Neill was terrified.

"But, of course!" the sister of Ali answered quietly. "God will."

CHAPTER VII

I

"*Il a ja cinc ans, ou mains*," Josselyn sang his interminable Romaunt of the Rose.

" *En mai estoie, ce songoie,*
" *El tens amoreus plain de joie*
" *El tens ou tote rien s'esgaie,*
" *Qui l'en ne voit boisson ne haie*
" *Qui en mai parer ne se voille*
" *El covrir de novele foille. . . .*"

" Five years have walked their destined
        way
" Since in the perfumed night of May
" I had this dream; in the moon of joy
" Whose magic puts on beauty as decoy
" For all of nature; when each shrub
        and brake
" Gaily their leafy garment take. . . ."

Yes, O'Neill thought, it might have been five years and not five months ago since he had been in Damascus with them all, so high a wall had arisen between that life and this. The whole thing had even been like a vision out of Josselyn's Romaunt. October was here now, and there was an end, thank God, to the heavy flies and foul stinks of the bazaars. The blue Moabite mountains seemed each day a little more like the mountains south of Dublin. . . . Jerusalem was quiet, with the deadly quietness of a man about to kill. The Arabs visiting the mosque of Omar, guaranteed in their pilgrimage by the Emperor, were finding it safer to wear shirts of chain armour, so free was the Temple with its daggers. The Temple was winning against the Sultan of Aleppo, and there was a rumour that the Old Man of the Mountain had been assassinated, and that the successor to him, the new Old Man, was not averse from making a secret treaty with the Grand Master. O'Neill smelt war. Only for the iron hand of the Emperor there would be war now. Ah, well, O'Neill wished it would come !

He was walking quietly behind a detachment of English troops, who were being taken out for some scouting practice in the highlands around Jerusalem, when he noticed a young Arab with his retinue reining into the wall, some young sheykh making his pilgrimage to the Noble Dwelling. The bowmen tramped stolidly by, O'Neill following them, when the Arab called to him with studied insolence.

"Ho! What-Is-Thy-Name! Cannot you stand still when an Arab gentleman goes by?"

O'Neill's face froze in anger at the insult. His teeth bared threateningly. He swung back his long kurbash. It hissed through the air on the back stroke with the hiss of a snake.

"O beater of women!" The Arab sheykh dropped the scarf from about his face, and O'Neill saw the sister of Ali smiling at him.

"Good God!" O'Neill said dumbfoundedly. And then quickly: "Cover your face, Kothra, in this town."

"Are you glad to see me?" she asked.

He came across and patted her mare on the neck. "How glad I can't tell you."

"Here are some folk you know," she turned to the followers, who were smiling and touching their foreheads to him. "And some you don't, but who, for all that, are your friends." He went amongst them, touching palms.

"Have you come to see the Noble Dwelling, Kothra?"

"To see that, and to see you, O'Neill, our friend. Is all well with you?"

"All is well with me. And with you?"

"All is well with me, and with the Bani Iskander. And I have messages for you, O'Neill, and presents."

"I'll give a few orders to my lieutenant," he said, looking after the bowmen, "and then I will be at your service, Kothra, and be your guide to the Noble Dwelling." As he went after the troop he motioned to the big Moor behind her. "Listen, Yussuf es-Senussi, it is not meet for the sister of Ali to show her face in this town. She must not be strong-headed. Do you understand me?"

The Moor nodded.

"Yes, sheykh, I understand."

II

He worried, now they were together, about
her being in Jerusalem. Though Emperor
Frederick had promised all Moslem folk
access to the Mosque of Omar, yet it was not
an invitation to be taken very seriously, for
Frederick was far away, and in El-Aqsa, the
Templars' Church, in the grounds of the
Noble Dwelling there were swords and knives
always with eager mouths for Moslem blood.
It was so easily explained that the visiting
Saracen had uttered filthiness about the Cross
of Christ, and that the assailant was being
disciplined by the Order. Also, O'Neill felt,
what influence he had was only with the
English troops in El-Kuds, the Holy, and
how long that would last he did not know.
Only the day before yesterday Sir Otho had
asked to see him, and when O'Neill had
walked into the hall of the old Saracen
house, into the pillared room with the floor
strewn with herbs, he found the Cornish
knight was not alone. Trelawney was sitting before a bottle of rhenish wine, but
the figure with him in the monk's robe and
cowl was sipping water. O'Neill noticed

the beautiful frail hand around the thin Venetian glass. Trelawney seemed ill at ease.

"My lord," the Cornish knight said, "this is Sir Miles O'Neill. Miles, the Grand Master wishes to put some questions to you."

"Sir!" Miles bowed.

The hooded figure threw the cowl back from his head, and Miles saw in front of him the face and eyes of the man whom the Saracens hated as they hated Satan who was stoned; the man whom both Pope and Emperor feared. He had an old frail face and soft beautiful white hair, and the pinched nose and mouth of the ascetic. The tonsure on his head was like polished ivory. He seemed like an old saint until you saw his eyes. His eyes were terrible. They were grey and seemed to have no pupil. It was as though you lifted your sight in reverence to see the soul in the Grand Master's eyes, and all you beheld were ovals of grey stone. It was as if the eyes of a statue had been put in the face of a man. When he began to speak his voice had the little tinkle of a silver bell.

CRUSADE

"Sir Miles, you must not think that because I have not seen you before you are unknown to me. I have heard much of the fights at Bethlehem and Rouge Garde, and your policing of the Sepulchre has been temperate and wise."

His voice was like a little melody, and had Miles only heard his voice, and seen his beautiful silver head, he would have thought it impossible that when this man spoke of the Impenitent Thief, he spoke of the Lord Jesus; that he was the most evil scholar of his day, knowing and practising black Cabbalistic rites; that it was his word that had assassinated the envoys of the Old Man of the Mountain on Saint Crispin's day, when they were returning after making peace with Richard Lionheart—they had come in friendship with their presents of crystal elephants and giraffes fashioned in crystal, and packets of ambergris, and games of chess, and with the blunt straightforwardness that Saladin loved the Lionheart had received them, and promised friendship with their Lord. But on their way homeward, from the depths of his Order, the Grand Master had struck. All this O'Neill would have disbelieved, hearing his voice. But all this he could not but believe now, seeing those dreadful eyes.

"You have been a prisoner in Damascus, Sir Miles?" the Grand Master asked.

"I have."

"And you doubtless know the city?"

"Very well, sir!"

"Now here we have luck," the Grand Master sipped his water, "for this Irish knight will tell us all we wish to know."

"My Lord," Miles said slowly, "I know of only one way of putting it, my blunt way. I shall tell you nothing."

"Now why should this be?" The voice of the Grand Master changed from the tinkle of the little bell to the purr of a cat. "Do you not, then, believe in the holy mission of Christ?"

"I do," Miles answered. "My Lord, do you?"

"Miles! Miles!" Trelawney pleaded. "My Lord, he is only a hot-headed Irish boy. He means no harm. I know them."

"There is something here not overt," the Grand Master seemed not to have heard

Miles' reply. "Why won't you tell us?" he asked.

"I was treated as a guest by the Saracen, and released from bondage out of their mercy. What sort of cur should I be to tell the secrets, if I knew any, of a generous foe?"

"Indeed! Sir Otho, cannot you do something to convince your lieutenant of the necessity of this information?"

"There are high policies, Miles," the Cornishman began, "of our Lord the King—"

"I know nothing of high policies," O'Neill was very cold. "But I think our Lord the King can forward those without a knight of his losing his honour. By God!" he swore hotly, "what shameful thing do you wish me to do? Sir Otho, I turn over the command to Josselyn. I had thought I would receive better at English hands."

The Cornishman flushed purple and stood up.

"You are too fast, boy. I had not known your ransom was unpaid. Grand Master," he turned to the ghost-like figure in the white robe, "my lieutenant is right. What he has learned under the circumstances it would be improper for him to say."

The Templar drew his cowl over his head. Now there was nothing to be seen of his face but his thin nose, his thin mouth, and his granite eyes. There was an air of finality about the gesture that was terrifying. Anything human about him was now gone. He was now the hooded Master of the Temple.

"Sir Miles is right," he said. His voice was cold as a cold freezing wind. "And yet Sir Miles advises himself ill."

"Sir, do you threaten me?" Miles looked at the prelate's eyes. There was a faint smile in them. Nothing could be more quiet than the Grand Master's face. But Miles looking down saw a terrifying thing. The beautiful ivory hands of the Grand Master were writhing as in torment. The ten fingers searched about like tentacles of a devil fish. They threshed like a nest of young serpents. One could almost imagine them hissing like venomous serpents.

"Yes," the Grand Master said quietly. "I threaten. Who will protect you?"

The Cornish knight rose in his chair, sat down; reached for his bottle and glass; drank a mouthful; spluttered; kept quiet. The Grand Master looked at O'Neill with his dreadful quiet smile in his stone eyes.

"Will not this protect me, Grand Master?" O'Neill touched with his finger-tips the Cross on his shoulder.

"I have seen so many who wore it," the prelate answered cynically, "gentlemen and rogues, fools and wise men, harlot-owners and saints. They are dead by swords in battle, or from daggers by stealth, from hunger and pestilence. I may shock you, but I have yet to see the Heavens opening and the Son of Man descending to protect His own."

"My only satisfaction, sir, is that I go to a Gentleman with my honour clean." He watched the curling fingers twisting with murder. The Templar caught his glance, and muffled his hands in his wide monk's sleeves.

"But it bores me," the Grand Master said shortly, " to talk to a dead man."

"Miles! Miles!" Trelawney pleaded. O'Neill raised his sword hand to his chin, and turning, walked out of the hall.

Like some dreadful cowled ghost the
Templar remained in his memory, but more
terrible still was the memory of the
shamed, perspiring face of the Cornish
commander.

CHAPTER VIII

I

THERE was always about her, wherever she went, faint perfume, a perfume of very cold water and little mountain flowers. When she walked by his side through the heavy *suqs* of Jerusalem, in whose crevices there still lurked the heat and stench of the summer that was dying, O'Neill felt a memory of the spring time that had been a dream, a spring time one feared would never come again. Fitter than the rimes of the Romaunt of the Rose Josselyn was ever singing seemed each gesture, each step. All in Jerusalem of the English knights and archers knew her to be a sheykh of the tribe that had captured O'Neill in battle, and tended him through sickness, and set him magnanimously free, and that he should show her what kindness was in his power they found only fitting.

CRUSADE

That she was a woman none knew, except perhaps Josselyn, who concealed, O'Neill was beginning to discover, beneath his casual manner and speech, a sound, wise head. Sir Otho Trelawney asked the young sheykh to meat with him, and Kothra accepted in her sweet dignity. O'Neill was afraid that at table the burly Cornishman would allow himself some masculine jests that might offend her, but soon the worried man rose, excusing himself, and leaving her to O'Neill and Josselyn. Trelawney's manner to O'Neill was one of pleading apology. He could not resent the words of the Grand Master to his lieutenant, seeing how the great secret designs he had in mind must dovetail with Temple ambitions. And he felt he had left his deputy without protection. O'Neill had told him: "I wish you wouldn't worry, sir!" But he worried all the more. Thinking to compliment O'Neill's guest, he gave her a beautiful Italian sword, which she accepted with grave courtesy. The following morning the Cornish knight received two great emeralds from the Caucasus for his lady, and a beautiful Nejd mare for himself. The Cornishman walked in to where Kothra and O'Neill and Josselyn were sitting. He had the emeralds in his hands.

"But I can't accept all this, young sir."

"My father, Sheykh Haroun, and myself, and my cousins Abdallah and Mohammad, have sent them to you for this reason," Kothra explained. "When Sheykh O'Neill was with us, we became fond of him, and we heard later that he arrived in Jerusalem penniless and worn—you will forgive me, dear O'Neill. And you took our friend in, sir, when he was in need. We are all friends, Arab and Christian, even though we battle. And that can be in a courteous sheykhly wise. Though O'Neill would not be of us, and hurried from our gardens and little rivers of Damascus to Jerusalem, yet we of Damascus and the desert esteem him much. And we wish to be friends with those who befriend him."

The Cornishman turned white and looked at the ground. Suddenly he rushed out of the room.

"But what have I done, O'Neill?" she asked in terror. "What have I said? Have I made some dreadful blunder? O dear God!" she all but cried. "I have insulted

him in some way, and he will think the
Arab are churls. O'Neill, my heart is
sore."

"No! No!" Miles comforted her.
"Listen, Kothra. It is the English way. He
is so overcome that he cannot find words.
That is all. He is very moved. That is
all."

"Is that what it is, O'Neill? I am glad.
He must love you so."

II

He told her: ' Kothra, I am going to
be a nuisance to you, but when you
make the *Ziyárah*, your pilgrimage to the
Rock, I am afraid I shall have to be with
you."

"You are no nuisance, O'Neill, and it will
have a sweetness to be near a friend while
praying.' That was all she said. He was
glad she asked no questions. He was no
good at lying, and to admit that in spite of
the Emperor's edict, no Arab sheykh's life
was safe, would have been dreadfully hard.
He walked by her side, two Welsh kerns
following them, as she put her right foot

delicately into the Noble Dwelling, murmuring the Moslem ritual: O Lord. pardon my sins, and open to me the doors of Thy mercy! They passed the lowering Templar sentinels at the door of the Mosque of Omar, and entered the building lovely with scrolled gold and Afghan tiles. In the shaded Cubbet the Eternal Rock slumbered, like the grey shoulders of some sleeping giant—the Rock which was the threshing floor of Ornan the Jebusite, and which to all Muslim is one of the Rocks of Paradise, and the centre of the world. On it on the Day of Resurrection the Angel Israfil will stand to blow the last trumpet. and beneath it is the source of every drop of sweet water that flows on the face of the earth.

"O God," Kothra prayed the prayer called Solomon's, "pardon the sinners who come here and relieve the injured."

She bent reverently at the "Footstep of the Prophet," where Mohammad mounted the beast Boraq, ascending into Heaven on the night of the miraj. She prayed at Bab el Jannah, where Elias prayed, and which is reputed to be the covering of Solomon's tomb. And in the cavern beneath the Rock she bowed reverently to the mark of Gabriel's fingers on the stone, and inclined to the great iron bar which is the sword of Ali ibn Abi Talib, the Lion of God. She left the great Mosque and saw the beautiful Dome of the Chain, standing by the greater Dome like a filly at foot. She came to the little Dome of the Ascent, and the beautiful pulpit of lace-like marble called the Prophet's Standpoint. With quiet reverential steps she visited the *Suq el Ma'rifah*, the market of Knowledge, near where David prayed. She saw the 'Mand 'Eisa, or Jesus' Cradle, and near the " Women's Mosque " she saw the Bir el Waraqah, or Well of the Leaf. And she was shown the column where Es Sirat, the bridge that joins heaven and hell, will start on the Day of Judgment. She looked eastward to where Dajjal, who is Antichrist, will appear and be stopped and baffled in his march on Jerusalem. And leaving the Noble Dwelling, she blessed the Lord Mohammad and murmured the customary prayer: O Lord, pardon my sins, and open to me the doors of Thy grace. And then, star-eyed and jasmin-faced, she looked up at O'Neill, and said: "Thank you, O'Neill!"

He shook his head. "Thank you, Kothra," he told her. And she laid her hand on his arm.

She had various visits to make to Arab families in the neighbourhood, and O'Neill's mind was wandering as he went down to Saint Sepulchre to go the rounds. He was to see her home, or rather to her cousins' at Bethlehem that evening, and it seemed strange to him to be going to the castle he had once helped to empty and hold. Only for that dreadful affair of de Lacy's he would never have known her. . . .

At David's gate, when the sun had fallen he met her with the great Moorish eunuch. The hunters' moon was just heaving up through the East. He passed her through the sentries, giving the counter-sign of the day. When they were out she turned to the Moor and said they were galloping ahead. But the Moor shook his head.

"The lady is under my guard from her father," he said firmly.

"But Yussuf, we all know Sheykh O'Neill."

"O sister of Ali," the Moor spoke out in the blunt old servants' way, "it is not right for a Moslem lady to ride with a Christian knight."

"Look Yussuf." She took her long jewelled dagger from her belt and handed it to O'Neill. "Now I am defenceless." She laid her hand on O'Neill's riding coat. "Look, Yussuf!" She turned to O'Neill. "*Dakheelak!*" she pleaded. "I come under your roof." She turned to Yussuf triumphantly. "Now, O father of fearfulness!" she said triumphantly. And the Moor could only laugh his chuckling negro laugh, shaking his head, and slapping his jelly-like thighs as they rode away from him.

They rode quietly down the moonlit night. Afar off the nomad shepherds' dogs made their loud barking, and the tinkle of camel bells from the paddocks set up a sound like crickets. They said nothing one to the other. They shared with each other the soft night of great moon and roaming hares. Half-way toward Bethlehem they came on an encampment of Provençal men-at-arms, probably a pilgrim guard from Aix. They were lying around a fire of olive-wood, while a ragged troubadour was declaiming to them.

"Gentlemen, burgher and tramp," he was half singing, half speaking:

CRUSADE

" March bare to the Holy War,
" Led from camp to desolate camp
" By Gautier Sans Avoir.
" Clear in my inner sight
" I see the arrow drawn,
" Against the giant Turkish knight
" By Godfrey de Bouillon."

The trouvere was a tall bony man with his heels showing bare in the firelight through his knitted hose above his Provençal pointed boots. His sword's edge peeped through the ragged sheath, and the plume in his hat was broken. He had a nose like a plough-share, and his left eye was half closed, and had a scar over it, probably from the blow of a tankard in a pothouse.

"What is he? What is he saying, O'Neill?" Kothra asked.

"He is a tinker poet, as we call them in Ireland, sister of Ali, and he is making a tavern poem about the first Crusaders, about King de Bouillon and Walter the Penniless. Come along."

"No! No!" Kothra insisted. The poet strutted before the soldiery, with his left hand on his sword. His good eye challenged the assembly.

ı' Not I to chronicle," he announced
　　in mock humility,
" In limping prosish phrase,
" Those deeds, a spectacle
" Of valour for all days.
" But who shall write in gold,
" For our children's children to pore
" These battles, now that old
" Blind Homer is no more!"

He stood as if stricken at the decline of
letters, while his eye and a half glittered with
the quick actor's glitter of the Southern
Frenchman. The bravos and ha-has of the
guard were as meat and wine to him.

"O'Neill," Kothra said suddenly, "look
at his poor stockings and his wretched hat.
O'Neill, how terrible!" She rode forward into
the light of the fire, and put her hand in her
waistband. "*Ya shâ'ir!*" "O poet!" she
called. O'Neill saw the twinkle of gold pieces
to the ground. The trouvere seemed to suck
them up with a quick swoop. His gesture
was the adept rapid gesture of a pick-pocket.
O'Neill rode into the firelight beside Kothra.
The men-at-arms looked at him and murmured
his name, standing up in respect. The travelling rimer's ear was cocked like a hawk's eye.

"Sit down, men! Sit down!" O'Neill told them quietly. He came close to Kothra, ready to take her away. He could already see visions of her adding the poet to the gazelle hound and lemur and honey-bear in the garden and he was quite certain the poet would not be good for the animals. The poet drew a deep breath:

" We have not forgotten yet
" That Western chivalry,
" Tancred and Plantagenet!
" No, nor the newer men,
" Who crossed the untamed snarling sea,
" To battle the Saracen.
" That shining angelic band
" Who hedge God's grave with steel.
" Rouge Garde and the savage stand
" Of the younger Miles O'Neill——"

The soldiers jumped to their feet shouting. Their hurras roused the dogs of the country-side. They stamped their feet, and whipped out their weapons and shook them in the air.

"For God's sake, Kothra, come on."

She had taken all the money from her waistband and flung it to the troubadour, and was tugging at her wrist. O'Neill caught her mare by the snaffle. He called to it by

G

name: "*Ya Umm es-saghyr*, O mother of the little one, trot!" But Kothra had thrown the poet her bracelet of ivory and fine gold, with little elephants scrolled on it in gold. "O silly one," he told her, when they were on the road again.

"But he is a *shâ'ir*, O'Neill, one that feeleth, and he had your name in his song. O, O'Neill, do you not know that this is what the Arabs cherish, to have the poets sing their names in songs?"

"But, Kothra, he never heard my name until to-night, when the soldiers mentioned it. That nose of his smelt bakshish as a hound's nose smells the fox."

"O no! O'Neill! How can you say that? Everybody knows your name. It is the business of poets to know names, yours and Tancred's and de Bouillon's."

"But, small Kothra, when the Father of the Nose took to poetry the world lost an eminent barber."

"You mustn't say that, O'Neill. You must not say anything against poetry. It is an art very difficult. And he was a good poet," she insisted stubbornly. "He knew all the great names: yours, Cœur de Lion's, everyone's."

CHAPTER IX

"O how dreadful is this place!" The voice of the Templar celebrant rang through El-Aqsa. "Truly this is none other but the House of God, and gate of Heaven."

"Alleluia!"

"I saw the Holy City, New Jerusalem, coming down from God out of Heaven, prepared as a bride for her husband." The priest read from his missal. The voices of the choir crashed into the ritual.

"How dreadful is this place! This is none other than the House of God, and the gate of Heaven. Surely the Lord is in this place and I knew it not.

"Alleluia.

"And when Jacob was now awakened, as one out of a deep sleep, he said:

"Surely the Lord is in this place, and I knew it not.

"Alleluia!

"Surely the Lord is in this place, and I knew it not.

"Alleluia!"

The clear voices of young boys took up the hymn, *Urbs beata Hierusalem*. Their voices were high and eager. They beat against the roof of El-Aqsa like the wings of birds.

"Holiness becometh thine house, O Lord!" said the priest at the altar.

"For ever and ever," answered the acolytes.

"Mine house, saith the Lord," rang one voice from the choir.

"Shall be called the house of prayer," the singing boys trilled.

"And Jacob rose early," chanted the priests, "and set up a stone for a pillar: and he poured oil thereon, and vowed a vow unto the Lord: Surely this place is holy, and I knew it not.

"Alleluia."

By the altar of El-Aqsa, a little aside, on a manner of throne, the Grand Master sat. His eyes were closed, so that one could only see the unearthly beauty of his face. Around him and beneath him sat the priests of the order of the Temple, aloof grim men, their eyes on their books, with the proper of the season, marked in quaint script and musical notation. The Celebrant at the altar was a young monk, who wore over his white Templar's habit a great cope of gold. Kneeling on the steps in their white surplices and black soutanes were the small altar boys. They had olive faces, and the high cheeping voices of sparrows. They were like small sparrows in a great net. The priests were burly fighting men, with the exception of the Grand Master, with his old poet's face—when the eyes were closed. Behind the congregation in the church the choir sang their plain chant, concealed by a great grille of ironwork.

"The foundations of this Temple hath God in His wisdom firmly grounded, wherein the Angels extol the Lord of Heaven: though tempests rage, they can never prevail against it, seeing it was founded upon a rock," went the antiphon.

"Alleluia!"

Here and there, in knots, in straggling parties, the congregation knelt or lounged against the vast pillars of the former Mosque. Pilgrims, their thick outland costume strange in contrast to the soft raiment of the native;

beggars, their foul sores dimmed in the shadow of the huge church; a visiting German princess with her train of heavy-headed, heavy-bellied officials; a Venetian statesman, his face pitted with treachery, attended by three boys, who seemed more like women than lads; a knot of free-lance soldiery, awed in the church of the great fighting order; hawkers of religious objects, their eyes seeking customers to assail at the finish of the service. And here and there a quiet, a too quiet, figure in native abbas and turban, with his hands up his sleeves, and his head bowed in devotion, but his wicked keen eyes swirling from right to left, from left to right.

The bell on the altar tinkled, and all knelt. They were now approaching the secret part of the mass. O'Neill pulled at Kothra's sleeve, and brought her to her knees. Josselyn closed up to her far side.

"O Adonay," went the Templar ritual—the voice of the officiant rose and fell in supplication, "and leader of the house of Israel, who appearedst in the Bush to Moses in a flame of fire, and gavest him the law in Sinai: Come and deliver us with an outstretched arm.

"O Root of Jesse, which standest for an ensign of the people, at whom kings shall shut their mouths, to whom the Gentiles shall seek: Come and deliver us and tarry not.

"O Key of David, and Sceptre of the House of Israel, that openest and no man shutteth, and shuttest, and no man openeth: Come and bring the prisoner out of the prison house, and him that sitteth in darkness and the shadow of death.

"O Dayspring, Brightness of Light everlasting, and Sun of Righteousness: Come and enlighten him that sitteth in darkness and the shadow of death.

"O King of the Nations, and their Desire; the Corner Stone who makest both one: Come and save mankind, whom thou formedst out of clay."

And now the bell gave another warning and all was silent. Through all the vast church was a sort of death. O'Neill had a chill in his heart. They might be calling on God, or they might be calling on One Other They might be celebrating Christ's arising out of death, or they might be celebrating the death itself. He felt Kothra clasp his forearm in fear. He looked around at her and smiled in reassurement. Out of his eye's edge he noticed Josselyn, watchful as a hound.

All through the service he had been bitterly reproaching himself for allowing Kothra to come, but she had so pleaded to see a Christian service that he could find no reason for refusal. He could not explain to her that he dreaded the Temple as much as he dreaded Hell. Indeed Hell he did not dread at all, but the cold grim quality, the almost diabolism of the order, gave his utter healthiness a sense of repulsion. And she had said: " O'Neill, you have come into our great Mosque at Damascus, el Jami' el Amawi, and you have been with me to the Dome of the Rock, and may I not come with you to your place? You know, O'Neill, how we of Syria love Mary's son, and it will be another bond of friendship between us; between you, O'Neill, and the Bani Iskander, Alexander's children, who love you. Please, O'Neill." He wanted her to come to Saint Sepulchre, where she could see the strange Copts with their golden clappers and golden bells, and the tonsured friars, and the Greeks with their black hats and copes of wrought silver and gold. There, in spite of occasional crudities, it was a refreshing, sane ceremony. They wept over Christ's death, and they were overjoyed at the Resurrection, and their hymns were gentle hymns, like *Jesu, Auctor Clementiae*, Jesus, of mercy Source alone: or *Martyr Dei, qui unicum*, Martyr of God, the Only Son; or *Lustra sex qui jam peracta*, Thirty years among us dwelling; not the mystic ritual of the Templars, with their *Angulare fundamentum*, or Cornerstone hymn. But she would have none of it. "But I do not want to go to a Sepulchre of One who never died. Cannot you see, O'Neill?"

"But the only other place is the Temple, the ancient Jami' el-Aqsa. You don't want to go there, Kothra."

"Yes, I want to go to the Temple, O'Neill."

He was frankly afraid to take her there, for though he knew Sir Otho was working hard to gloss over his disagreement with the Grand Master of the Templars, yet he felt that, whatever Sir Otho did, his life would never again be safe in Jerusalem. Beneath his short maroon woollen coat, with the Crusader symbol over his heart, he wore now a finely-knit coat of Damascene mail.

He was placing a small Irish knife under his armpit, in addition to the heavy curved blade concealed under his coat, when Josselyn knocked at his door and strolled in. The Kentish boy watched him closely.

"Pleasant sort of dress for Sunday," he murmured.

"I'm going to the Temple of the Lord," O'Neill grinned.

But Josselyn didn't smile at all. He picked up a small steel mirror and looked at himself in it. "Do you think it wise?" he asked O'Neill.

"I don't," O'Neill answered.

"I think I'll come along," Josselyn said quietly.

"I think you won't," O'Neill was firm. "This little row of mine is none of your business. You keep out."

"Are you taking our young Arab friend with you?"

"Yes," O'Neill nodded. "She—he wants to see it, or else I shouldn't go."

"Then I'll come along," Josselyn said.

"You won't," O'Neill told him firmly.

"Good God! Do you think I can't take care of myself and my guest?"

"Then I'll follow you." Josselyn was stubborn. "Miles, don't be silly. I'll be there anyhow. You may as well let me come with you."

"All right," O'Neill said diffidently. But he was relieved to know that Josselyn was on Kothra's left hand side. The marigold haired man of Kent was like a Viking of old time. The terrific bodily strength of him and sound heart and mind were a bulwark. . . .

" *Ite, missa est:* " the officiant had finished his secret prayer. "Go! It has been sent."

The preacher of the day, a huge black-jowled knight, in white cassock strode on to the altar. He knelt clumsily and kissed the Grand Master's hand. He turned from the Grand Master, and knelt at the altar an instant, as if praying. He rose and strode to the pulpit. He hitched at the cord of his habit, as though it were a sword-belt. With every step he came down firmly on his heels, with his soldier's step. He had an iron mouth, and black iron eyes. He sprang up the pulpit steps, and leaned on the pulpit rail, as if reviewing men-at-arms.

When he spoke he spoke as if issuing words of command.

"Zachariah," he snapped out, "the first chapter, verses eight to ten:

"I saw by night, and beheld a man riding upon a red horse, and he stood among the myrtle trees that were in the bottom, and behind him were there red horses, speckled and white:"

Josselyn leaned over Kothra's shoulder and touched O'Neill. "Look out!" his eyes sent a warning. Miles glanced around. He could see nothing. The nearest person to him was a lay Templar brother, with meek downcast face, and iron grey beard, his hands in his sleeves. The brother was paying no attention to anything but the preacher's sermon.

"Then said I, O my lord, what are these? And the angel that talked with me said unto me, I will show thee what these be." There was a dreadful sneer in the preacher's tones.

"And the man that stood among the myrtle trees answered and said, These are they whom the Lord hath sent to walk to and fro through the earth."

So quickly did it happen that O'Neill could hardly follow it all. Josselyn said:

"Miles!" sharply. O'Neill turned in time to see the lay brother fling himself forward knife in hand. O'Neill knew the knife was not for him, but for the sister of Ali, and stepping behind her received the blow on his shoulder blade. The blow was the savage blow of a little hammer, and there was a sting like the sting of a wasp. There was a tinkle of broken glass as the blade shivered on the links of steel. The hilt dropped on the marble tiles.

"Ye will read further in the vision of the son of Berechiah, the son of Iddo the prophet: Thus saith the Lord of Hosts: I am jealous for Jerusalem and for Zion with a great jealousy."

Josselyn had the lay brother by the throat. O'Neill could hear the man's short breath coming through his nose. There was a heavy crunch as the Kentish man smashed the monk's head against a pillar. O'Neill took Kothra by the sleeve.

"Come," he told her.

She looked at him in amazement. So quietly, so quickly had all occurred that she had seen and heard nothing.

"But O'Neill—"

"I said: Come. Follow Josselyn." He was brusque. He slipped the small Irish knife in his hand, and pushed her before him. They passed the huddled figure beside the column. They picked their steps quietly along the wall through seated and standing worshippers, and walked out through the sentried portals. They walked quietly through the Noble Dwelling, until they came to the Dome of the Rock. They strolled along the marble platform, and through the massive gates into the street. There came a burst of singing from the Church el-Aqsa.

"They adorned the face of the temple with golden coronals: and dedicated the altar unto the Lord.

"Alleluia!"

"But they haven't finished," the sister of Ali turned to O'Neill, "and I wanted to see it all, O'Neill. O'Neill, it is such bad manners to leave a mosque abruptly."

O'Neill laughed. He laughed quietly for minutes, a laugh that was not humour but relief. Josselyn cursed heartily in English. His face was red and furious. He looked back at the Temple with cold fury in his eyes. Kothra looked at them aghast, as if both had suddenly gone mad.

"O, O'Neill," she said suddenly, and her white face became whiter, and her eyes full of fear, "there is a great cut in your coat. And there is a great coin of blood on your shoulder. And you are wearing mail, O'Neill. O what does it mean? I am afraid. I am so afraid."

CHAPTER X

I

HE could not but laugh at himself with surprise, and perhaps with a little bitterness, that, prepared by temperament and calling for anything of death, where now a problem of life faced him he was helpless. He had been brought up to a certain way; sent on a certain mission. Down the marked roadway of his years he had gone unthinking, but now he must, as it were, cross country to no settled point, and he did not know what to do.

One thing was certain. He could no longer stay in Jerusalem, nor in the Holy Land, nor in any place where the Temple stretched its dark shadow. He was utterly a dead man, in so far as the Templars were concerned. Ireland he could not go back to. There was nothing in Leinster for him, and the small fighting in the Ulster hills would be ridiculous to him now he had been a captain in the East. Nor might Blind Hugh have him. A certain dark and passionate Irishness sprang up in him to see himself so lone and deserted now. He thought bitterly: why should such a great organization as the Templar order attack a poor captain of foot soldiers, one utterly unimportant. But, he figured shrewdly: alive you are unimportant, O'Neill, but dead you are of great value. Then it will be remembered that you were the inner guard of Saint Sepulchre, and a grand-nephew of the King of Ulster. But he was against the Temple, the Order will hint, and now, they would quote, "I shall behold man no more: with the inhabitants of the world. Mine age is departed and removed from me as a shepherd's tent." At first he had said: "Let them kill me, by God!" And now he said: "I'm damned if they shall."

Although he knew Sir Otho could do nothing, that in protecting him the Cornish knight would be risking his mission, he could not forbear from hurting him. When he turned over his command, he would accept nothing from the Duke's envoy but his exact pay. The burly man's face was white and shamed.

"Miles," Trelawney said, "I am, in England, close to our Lord the King, and I have in mind the writing of a letter—"

"Dear sir," O'Neill said silkily, "if one so close to His Majesty cannot protect his lieutenant what can the King's Majesty do? Also, Sir Otho, my small military gifts from now on will be directed against your lord the King." He did not mean that. But he felt an Irish turbulence boil through the gloss of chivalry.

"Miles, I am dreadfully sorry!" The Cornishman's shame was pitiable. But the Irishman was hard and cold.

"I should damned well think you would be."

Josselyn had been the unwilling witness of the interview. He had turned his back and was examining a little Syrian chaplet of amber, as though he had never seen anything like it before. Only when the Cornish knight left did he turn around.

"Miles, you know," he said embarrassedly,

"the old man can't do anything. And he's broken under it."

"I know," O'Neill said, "and I can't keep my anger down. It's my black Irish heart, Josselyn. My head tells me all this. But I turn bitter within, and the tongue strikes. I can't help it. It really hurts me more than it does him."

"Damn all politics, old captain, Josselyn said. "Now to get you out What about to-night?"

"No, I won't leave Jerusalem until I've seen the party from Damascus clear on their way home."

"Miles, you're mad. You're alone here, except for me. And they've got all the Mohammedan world to protect them. And every minute counts."

"They'll go in two days. I won't go until they're gone."

"You're mad. You're utterly mad. But you're right," Josselyn grinned.

II

O'Neill had told the sister of Ali a cock-and-bull story of a monk whom he had ejected from the Sepulchre for quarrelling with the Greeks, and who had sworn to kill him, as an explanation for the attack in the Temple. And had later in the day told her, to quiet her fears for him, that the man had been locked up as a madman. Miles knew why she had been attacked. The Templars wanted him to feel that his protection was of no value, and to hurt him before they killed him Very probably, too, they knew, as they seemed to know everything, that this was no young Arab sheykh, but a girl. God! he swore, why had she come to El-Kuds the Holy? If she weren't in the neighbourhood, he would have been well on his way to Cyprus by now, looking up his old chief, de Lacy. And yet, even at the risk of his life he was glad to have seen her again. It was a memory to keep for the black days coming, and he knew there would be black days. And now she was in danger, too, through him. He sought out the black swordsman, Yussuf, and told him the truth of the attack in the Temple: that it was made on Kothra, not on him The negro's face was like black stone. When he said he was lucky enough to catch the blow on his shoulder the African fanatic seized his hand and kissed it. And again the face became like black stone.

"So don't let her out of your sight, Yussuf, and for God's sake, get her back to Es-Sham at once."

"She shall never leave my sight by day, Sheykh O'Neill," Yussuf es-Senussi answered, "and at night this old dog shall watch outside her door."

"Remember, soon to Damascus!"

It came to him now with a shock that he was intensely fond of this country he was leaving. Never again to see the sweet proportions of the Noble Dwelling; and the little hills that are about Jerusalem, with their small wild flowers; the absurd gait of camels; the silver olive trees and their presses for oil; the blue hills of Moab, behind which one felt the vast wilderness of Sinai; Galilee of the sunshine and the great roach: whose eastern bank was so good for hunting bear, leopard, hyæna, and an occasional lion; the vast starry skies of Asia, whose great stars were like little lamps in a shrine; the surf breaking at Jaffa: the cotton fields beyond the town; the orchards heavy with apricots! Though he fought in Hungary or High Germany or Spain, yet it would be only straight-forward hacking, and the life would be only existence. There would be no subtlety to it. The men who wrote from right to left in beautiful curves and minute exact points, and had a vast courtesy—he would miss them. Asia Minor had taken the place of Ireland in his heart, and now was a second exile. The Arab story-tellers were like the Irish ones, the Arab dogs were like the coursing hounds of Ireland, and life, except for passionate gusts of religion and war, as in Ireland, flowed by softly and gently, as in Ireland too. Even the names of places had a significance like the Irish place names. Some of them the Tewkesbury friar who was learned in Hebrew had translated for him, and they were each like little poems: Carmel, the Field of Fruit; Bethlehem, the House of Bread; Bethacherem and Bethphage, the House of Vineyards, and the House of Figs, and Beth-haggan, the House of Gardens; Engannim, the Garden of Springs; Nahal-eshcol, the Valley of Grapes. Since he had put Ireland away, Asia had flowered in his heart.

However, there was too much to do to leave time for repining. Once on the deck of some

Greek merchant's boat, going to Cyprus for wine, he could think all he liked of his second lost country. But the job in hand was to get aboard, alive. While he was making his plans, Josselyn dropped in on him.

"I thought I might as well tell you," the Kentish boy smiled, "that a courier of the old man's has just left for England. He is to make arrangements for horses at each stage to be ready on the King of England's business, and for a sloop to be waiting at Jaffa."

"No, Josselyn," O'Neill said, "I won't accept it from the old man."

"It's not from the old man."

"Well, I can't afford it."

"You can damned well afford to let your old comrades help you. No, it isn't I alone. It's a half dozen of us. We're not going to go around to see you butchered in Jerusalem. Now, listen, you're to go around as if nothing had happened. When you see the Damascus party off across the Jordan ford, I shall escort them with the Welsh archers. When we get back, you slip out that night. You sit down and ride, O'Neill. There's no need to tell you how fast you've got to ride."

O'Neill laughed uncomfortably. "I don't know what to say. I'm ashamed of how I feel. I didn't think, outside yourself, Josselyn, I had a friend in the world."

"You've got hundreds here, so don't be a fool. Now, please do something for me. Young Hugh à William wants to go with you as squire. He's a good lad. His people are decent Welsh folk, and he'd get his knighthood in a few years. You'll like him, O'Neill."

"But I'm the poorest of poor knights, Josselyn. And God knows where I'm going. I'm sorry, but I can't take him."

"You've got to. He's gone with the King's Messenger and is waiting for you at Jaffa at the English Hospice. Remember, go around as if nothing had happened. But wear your chain shirt, and if you've got— any of the Damascus visitors with you, keep out of a crowd. For God's sake, keep out of crowds."

III

She came with the giant African attendant to pay some of her last visits, and O'Neill

met her at David's Gate. The Arab grooms
held the horses while they dismounted, and
they listened awhile to a story-teller who was
relating the epic of Taj al-Mulúk and the
Princess Dunyâ: "Now when Taj al-Mulúk
looked about him at the caravan, he saw a
handsome youth in neat attire and of shapely
make, with flower-like forehead and moonlike face, save that his beauty was wasted
and yellow lines had overspread his cheeks
by reason of parting from her he loved, and
great was his groaning and moaning, and
the tears streamed from his eyelids, and he
repeated several couplets of the poem called
'Longsome in Absence,' and when he had
ended them, he fell down in a fainting fit, and
coming to himself he recited the poem:
'Beware her Glance,' and he sobbed a loud
sob and swooned away. . . ."

She looked at O'Neill with a puzzled
humorous glance. "Is there love like that
among the Nasarenes, O'Neill?"

"No, only among the Arab, sister of
Ali."

"Now, God confound you, O'Neill!" she
turned on him furiously. "Do you know so
little of the Arab as that? Do you think the

Companions of the Prophet loved that way?
Or Saladin? Or Nureddin? Or Abd el
Malik, the Lion? Or Haroun er-Rasheed,
the Upright? Or Abu Tor, the Father of
the Bull? Do you think that I should give
myself to one melting like a rotten apricot?
Ah, but you laugh, O'Neill. You do not
mean this thing. But you must not make
me angry. Anger is unbecoming in a sheykh,
and these are my last two days in this place.
To-day and to-morrow."

"Then you leave for Damascus?"

"We leave Jerusalem for Damascus."

He was about to say "Thank God!" but she
was watching him closely, and he uttered
some banality of how he should miss her.
They walked around the walls, looking toward
the little hills of the Moabite country, past
the great stone houses where once Moslem
princes had lived. Only an occasional shambling beggar passed them, or a woman bearing
on her head a jar of water from a well.
Behind them the vast African trod, with his
strange un-African tread, on the balls of his
feet, agile as a leopard, light as a cat.

"When are you coming to Damascus to
see us, O'Neill?"

"Soon," he said. "Very soon." He was surprised he could lie so well, seeing how heavy his heart was that he would never see the marble city, with its fountains and gardens any more. Never again see the balls of gold in the glossy orange trees, or the almond trees breaking into a foam of beauty.

"You must come soon, O'Neill. For the Bani Iskander hunger to see their friend. Even the slaves of the house ask for you. And my father says: If Ali had lived, I should have liked the Sheykh O'Neill to be his friend. When he mentions Ali, O'Neill, his heart is bare. So that you see how he loves you. Also this, Mohammad and Abdallah, who know the wastes of the desert better than any other chiefs, say that the Khorezmians are massing in the north to come down on Syria and Palestine They are like the infinite locusts, thick as rain— yellow as locusts. And under their leader El-Wahsh, the Beast, they have sworn to leave no Mussulman or Christian alive, and to raze Es-Sham, the Beautiful, to the ground. Myself, I do not believe this thing. For has not Damascus seen the beginning of time, and will it not see time's end? But the people of the country are afraid of El-Wahsh. Listen, O'Neill, I will tell you a secret terrible thing. The King of the Assassins, the Sheykh el-Djebal, sent two of his best *fedawi*, or 'devoted ones', to kill El-Wahsh. But the Beast discovered them, and lopped their hands and feet off, and chained them by the neck to the pegs of his tent as dogs, and when he tired of that, he sent them to the kennels among the nomad hounds, so that not even the smallest bone of them remains. So Abdallah and Mohammad say: If you wish to see Damascus, come soon. To myself this is an incredible thing. But come soon, O'Neill. Listen, O'Neill, we will make an appointment now."

"I can't make an appointment now, Kothra, but listen, I will write."

"I wonder why you are lying to me," she said calmly. "I have been taught: a lie is a shameful stratagem. I do not think you want to come to Damascus to see us any more. And I think, too, you are unhappy I have come to El-Kuds." She faced him calmly. "There is a lot in this I do not like, and I do not understand, O'Neill."

"I do not swear, I just tell you, sister of Ali, that your coming to this bloody place has made me happy." He searched under his coat for a small parcel he had brought. "Now we are quarrelling, and it is not like the old days when we quarrelled. For then we were not friends, and it did not matter. But now we are friends, and it does. By God! Kothra, I will not be unfriends with you."

"Will you go aside, Yussuf," she asked the negro guard, "and let the sheykh explain." But the African shook his head.

"No!"

"Do you think then the sheykh will offer me insult?" She whipped with her voice.

"No."

"Are you afraid that this poor beggar," she pointed to a shambling figure who was following them on the off chance of a coin, "will hurt me?"

"Perhaps."

"Now God protect you, Yussuf," she said with dreadful coldness, "but you will answer to me for this impertinence."

"I will answer to you for anything, sister of Ali, in Damascus."

CRUSADE

O'Neill was undoing the parcel the Metropolitan of the Abyssinians had sent him as a present on his turning over command of Saint Sepulchre to Josselyn. He took out a scarf of green silk, so delicate that it could be rolled in two hands, and yet so big it would make a shawl for a woman. On it some Abyssinian craftswoman had wrought in red African gold a procession of the animals going into Noah's great ship. There was the great crocodile with the yawning mouth, and the clumsy rhinoceros, and the tiger, and the elephant, and deer with huge horns, and the tall giraffe, and huge baboons. And Noah's vessel had vast lateen sails, and Noah's sons stood on the deck of the boat, while the admiral's self peeped from a hatchway. Afar off the waters were rising in billows of red gold. A childish and very beautiful thing. The little princess who had wrought it was dead two centuries ago, the prelate had said, and yet one could imagine the deft brown fingers, her curious child's mind, could almost hear her sweet, low laughter.

"That is for me?" Kothra asked.

"Yes, that is for you.'

She took it and looked at it with eyes mirroring a deep wonder. "How lovely!" she cried, and held it to her bosom. "I have been angry and abominable while you were there with such a sweet gift," she said in swift distress. "How can you ever like me again, O'Neill?"

"It won't be very hard," O'Neill laughed.

She slipped the scarf from her chin and mouth, and held it over her arm while she wound the quaint Abyssinian shawl in its place under her head-dress. "Here, O thou!" she called to the shambling beggar, He sidled craftily up. "For thy harem, O Father of Misfortune," and she tossed him the scarf she had been wearing.

"By God, no!" O'Neill stepped forward and took it from him and was feeling in his pocket for a coin. Yussuf took one step forward, and his great curved knife, keen as a razor, heavy as an axe, was at the beggar's throat.

"Yussuf, you are of a surety mad," the sister of Ali called to him. "O, the poor beggar man!"

"Be quiet, Kothra," O'Neill said simply. He recognized in the man's poise the tensed body ready to rush and strike. "I think I'll have a look at this one," he murmured. "Yussuf, if he moves, cut his throat."

The man didn't move, but his eyes threatened. They were dreadful as the eyes of snakes. O'Neill yanked the turban from his head, and grinned as he saw the tonsure beneath. "If I stripped you, I'd find the Templar girdle beneath your rags, wouldn't I, brother?"

The Templar would not answer. He only glared at O'Neill with his baleful eyes. Yussuf looked meaningly over the battlements.

"Shall I?" he asked, "and throw him over. Your lordship can take the young sheykh down the street."

"It isn't worth it," O'Neill decided. "His two companions are probably waiting in another place. Go, brother. Try something a little less obvious the next time."

"There walks," O'Neill watched the man go down the street, head high and step firm, "there walks what was once a gentleman."

Kothra laid her hand on his shoulder and felt the chain armour beneath his tunic.

"I don't understand," she said. "I know you don't want me to understand, either, or you would tell me, O'Neill. O but, dear God! I wish Abdallah and Mohammad were here."

"You are all right in Bethlehem, Kothra. Nobody will do you hurt there. And you have Yussuf with you. You need no more protection."

"I! Do you think I care! Do you think I am afraid? I am afraid for you, O'Neill. If only my two cousins were here."

"If the sister of Ali will remember," Yussuf's mouth spread into a wide grin, "the first raid on Bethlehem, and the death of the Tartar captain at Rouge Garde. Also this," he said sternly, "God abhors daggers in the dark."

"The Compassionate, the Compassionating, Blessed be He!" She touched her forehead with her fingers. "Still, I wish Abdallah and Mohammad were here."

"As to me, Kothra," O'Neill smiled, "I wear a coat of mail. I am armed like a

Venetian bravo." He twirled his commander's whistle on its silver chain. "And there are five hundred Welsh and Cornish men in the Holy City."

"I know, but if Abdallah and Mohammad ——"

IV

He had been all morning, and now for some hours of the afternoon, paying small visits to friends, and settling up debts he owed, and was coming out of the Saddlers' Alley, half ashamed, half bothered. He had been invited to spend the night at Bethlehem by the Baron whom he had helped to dispossess for a short time, and the strangeness of the situation embarrassed him. That night he would sleep there, and in the morning Josselyn would pick up himself and the Damascus party and they would all ride to the Jericho ford. He had not seen the Lord of Bethlehem since the day de Lacy and he had tramped into his castle, and though he knew no reference would be made to that occasion, and that he would be welcomed as the friend of the Bani Iskander, yet it was a dreadful situation. It had taken all Kothra's persuasion to make him come.

"All that is over," she had said. "It is that way with the Arab. They understand. One acts under compulsion, seeing Destiny is what it is. And it was good for the Lord of Bethlehem. He'll take more care of his castle now."

"I can't go, Kothra."

"But if you don't come, O'Neill, he will think you are revengeful; that you are meditating a further *ghrazzu* on his place, and for that reason you will not eat his bread and salt. O'Neill, you are not thinking of another raid on my cousin's house?"

"Dear God! No!" O'Neill said indignantly.

"Then you must come."

"All right. I'll come."

"I'm glad. My father will like that."

"I'll ride over after your evening prayer."

"That is an arranged thing, O'Neill."

He thought, now that the afternoon was half-way past, he would go to his and Josselyn's lodgings and get two or three hours' sleep. There would be little sleep at Bethlehem, with their Arab love of

staying up half the night, while Greek
dancers and musicians entertained the parting guests. And after the ride toward
Jordan in the morning and back before
nightfall, by night again he would be
galloping on his way to the coast. It would
be hard work, this running away, harder
than fighting. He turned to pass Saint
Sepulchre on his way to the Damascus
gate.

"Don't walk so fast, O'Neill. I can't
catch you up."

He turned around quickly, and saw her.
She was walking along after him, in man's
riding dress. She had vast baggy breeches,
and small red shoes, and from underneath
the tassels of her head-dress her eyes
looked at him with a faint mockery. Her
waist-band was of twisted green silk, and
she wore a short Syrian jacket of green
and gold.

"Where's Yussuf?" he asked.

"I escaped Yussuf," she smiled, and
tapped her breeches with her riding switch.
She was very much the young gallant
of Damascus. Her dress of a young
Arab blood, and her little swagger were

strange in the precincts of the surly Sepulchre.

"I slipped down when all the house was drowsing after noon meal, and saddled the grey *Sabiqah*, 'that outrunneth'. And Yussuf did not see me at all."

"But why, Kothra, why did you come?"

"For this, O'Neill. I thought you might be uneasy, coming by yourself to my cousin's house. And if I led you there, you would be more happy. Also," she said, "I was glad to get rid of Yussuf. He follows me like a familiar spirit. He is mad on this: that Jerusalem is a dangerous place. Also, O'Neill, I wished to have news of you, that you were alive and unharmed."

"Come." O'Neill was brusque. "I'll get my horse and we'll ride to Bethlehem at once. Where did you leave the *Sabiqah*?"

"At David's Gate with the Arab lad. But O'Neill, must we rush away? It is the last time we—I shall be in El-Kuds, oh for so long! And if we just go down the booths, surely none will bother us there."

"Listen, Kothra. I shall be happy when we are on the high road, riding together, seeing the sun go down."

They walked along the quiet streets, loud only with doves. Near Caiaphas' House a detachment of Italian pilgrims, with a guard of three lean swordsmen were visiting the *Via Dolorosa*, the Painful Road to Calvary. An Arab beggar, with the huge swathed legs of leprosy, hobbled swiftly after them on T-shaped sticks.

"It will be like the night we rode to Bethlehem, under the full moon, and we met the broken poet. O'Neill, he was a very good poet, for all that you say," she added maliciously.

"*Irham ya Rabb! khalqak, alltheena anta khalaqta!*" the beggar was howling. "Have mercy, O Lord God, upon Thy creature which Thou createdst." The pilgrims looked up in mild surprise. The Milanese swordsmen seemed bored. "*Irham el-masakîn, wa el-juaanîn, wa el-iryanîn! Irham ya Allah!* Have mercy on the poor, the hungry, the naked! Have mercy, O God!"

She turned quickly round at the cry of distress, and faced the leper. Her fingers went into her waistband where she kept her gold coins. "Come hither, O Father of

Afflictions," she called. A head-dress of sack-cloth covered the man's possibly dreadful face He hobbled nearer.

Then the beggar did a dreadful thing.

The crutches dropped from his hands. He stood up, a whole man. His hand shot out and caught the top of the sister of Ali's silken shirt. There was the whine of torn silk. He ripped it open to the waist-band. She looked at him with eyes that had gone mad with shock and anger. Quietly, with lean white hands, he lifted the sack-cloth head-dress from his face. His head was tonsured. His face was lean and clean.

"Come down and sit in the dust, O virgin daughter of Babylon, sit on the ground, there is no throne," he sneered. "Thy nakedness shall be uncovered, yea, thy shame shall be seen!" He turned to the pilgrims. "Here is a soldier of the Cross whose darling is a woman of the Arab." He turned to the three Milanese swordsmen. "It is in Amos: all sinners of my people shall die by the sword."

The swordsmen shuffled, hesitated. Quietly,

with a dreadful anger in her eyes, Kothra was covering her bared bosom.

"I am Brother Renier de Sergines," the monk said quietly, "of the Order of the Templars."

The swordsmen half unsheathed their weapons. A terrible cold trembling came over O'Neill. He caught the monk by the shoulder and pushed him against a door. With dreadful deliberation he drew a long poniard from his belt.

"I will give you another little text, Brother Renier de Sergines, of the Order of Templars," he looked smilingly at the monk. "Hell from beneath is moved for thee to meet thee at thy coming." And he nailed the man by the throat to the wood of the door.

He stepped back and looked at the swordsmen. "And now, men, when you are ready." And he drew out his long weapon.

They looked at the dead monk, sprawled against the door, his head hideously sideways, his arms flopped like the arms of a scarecrow, and their faces became yellow, and they turned away. O'Neill slipped his tunic off and threw it around Kothra. He stood for a minute with drawn sword and shining coat of mail.

"Come," he told the girl.

"Do you think we can get to Bethlehem?" she asked. "I am not afraid. I am only asking."

"Not yet," he told her as he led her down the bye-street. "We will get to the convent of the Abyssinians. They are friends of mine, the men of Prester John. We will take refuge there."

V

He often thought, on the nightmare ride toward Château Neuf, of the unquestioning hospitality of the Abyssinians. When they arrived at the convent the Greek service in the Sepulchre was beginning, so that the big square was empty. The sound of the priests' chanting filled the close. He rapped at the door with the hilt of his sword, and the porter opened his eyes wide at the sight of the young Syrian sheykh, and the former captain of the Sepulchre with mail coat and bared sword.

"I wish to see His Beatitude," O'Neill explained, "and at once." When the old shaven-headed prelate came with his young secretary, O'Neill felt a sense of shame. They were all so frail, these priests of Abyssinia, and he was so strong, and Kothra was of one of the greatest of the Saracen tribes, and yet it was to the shadowy black man they had to appeal for protection.

But the old prelate never wavered. "You are our friend and under our roof, and being under our roof are under the roof of Prester John," he said quietly. "We are but poor simple monks," he said, "but what we have is yours." Only when he mentioned the tearing of Kothra's blouse did the old abbot and the young secretary look at each other with dismay, and O'Neill remembered that since the Abyssinians had once come to Jerusalem no woman had ever entered their holy house.

"God, sir!" he said. "I never thought—"

"You thought only that the Abyssinians were your friends, and that was beautiful and true. And that women have never entered our house," he smiled at Kothra, "is only old monks' crankiness. The Way came to us through the Holy Philip, who baptised the chief eunuch of Queen Candace. Also, it will not harm us to have a daughter in our house."

"Our little daughter will rest now," he said, and ringing his stringed Egyptian bell, he sent her off with an old priest. He took O'Neill's hand. "I am sending secretly for your English friend," he told O'Neill.

"For Josselyn."

"For Sir Josselyn."

The abbot took his other hand.

"He whom you have sent there is before the Judgement Seat of God," the old man said quietly. "Come into the convent chapel, my son, and kneeling silently, give evidence, and your old friend will go with you. Come. . . ."

When he returned Josselyn was there. Kothra was present, too. The priests had given her an amice of green and gold, which she wore instead of her torn blouse. She handed O'Neill back his coat. "Thank you, O'Neill," she said quietly.

"Well, Josselyn," O'Neill said. "I seem to have done it."

"Yes," the Kentish man smiled grimly, "you've done it. But he wanted it. He got it. The thing now is to get you two out."

"If we can get to Yussuf and my friends," Kothra said. But Josselyn flushed crimson. Kothra looked at him steadily.

"If you knew, Sir Josselyn, how weary I am of secrecy and lies. I can see something has happened to Yussuf. Is he in prison or dead?"

"Dead."

"Yussuf would prefer that. And Ferdous, and Mahanna ibn Mahjil, and Akhu et-Thi'b, the Wolf's Brother?"

"Dead," Josselyn told her. "Yussuf was looking for something in the Noble Dwelling and came in armed and the sentries killed him, and the others rode into a band of Hungarian archers who took them for marauders."

She looked at Josselyn steadily.

"There can nothing happen but by the permission of Allah!" she said proudly. "But Yussuf taught me horsemanship, and Ferdous and the Wolf's Brother, they will be missed in the jerids, the javelin plays, of Damascus, and Mahanna married my foster-sister but six weeks ago, and she is with child. Nevertheless, nothing occurs but by the ordinance of God."

She stood up proudly, but in an instant she was in tears, and the old prelate had her in his arms, sobbing against his shoulder. The abbot motioned O'Neill and Josselyn to leave them. The men walked on tip-toe out of the room. . . .

They left the Abyssinian convent at nightfall dressed in the robes Josselyn had brought, of a Templar knight and his page. They galloped up to the Damascus gate.

"Open!" O'Neill roared.

"Who calls?" The officer of the watch appeared, a little shabby and tired.

O'Neill tapped the big red cross on his mantle.

"This calls. On the Service of the Order."

"If your lordship will but give the counter-sign."

"'Thou art beauteous and comely, O daughter of Jerusalem,'" O'Neill whispered the secret special text, "'and terrible as an army in array for battle.'"

"Open the gates, there," the officer commanded. "Good hunting, my lords!" O'Neill

felt a shiver go through him. If the guards
knew it was the hunted, and not the hunters
who were passing!

They dropped their hands on their horses'
necks and giving them their heads, raced for
Mohammarie. The moon was rising, and
the road seemed good. O'Neill wondered
how Josselyn was getting on. Two hours
before, dressed in O'Neill's clothes and with
a Welsh kern in the robes of a young Arab
sheykh, the Kentish knight had started for
the Jordan ford, sure he would draw the pursuit after him. How far had they been allowed
past Bethlehem? O'Neill judged that the
Templar pursuit would not close in on them
until after midnight. When it did, Josselyn
would disclose himself as in the service of
the Duke of Cornwall, on an errand to Jericho.
If all went well the Templars at Jerusalem
would not know of his escape until early
morning, nine or ten o'clock.

They galloped through Mohammarie in
the full moon, the village dogs barking and
racing at their heels. Half-way toward Bethel
they were to meet a Syrian merchant of
Beyrout who was on his way to Nablus.
His tent was to be pitched by the highroad,

and he was to have a second disguise ready.
O'Neill's eyes had opened in wonder when
Josselyn had told him that Sir Otho was
placing the Duke of Cornwall's organization
at his command. He had only known the
military end of it. He had no idea of the
network of intrigue that spread over Lesser
Asia, woven beside the quiet lily-bordered
Thames.

He glanced at Kothra sitting quietly in
her saddle. He admired the easy seat and
unstirring hands. Oh, she could ride, the
sister of Ali! He wondered when she would
tire.

"If you are wondering when I will tire,
O'Neill," she answered his unspoken question, "don't think of it. I shall not tire
before you. Not that I am as strong, but
that I am bred to the saddle." She was
silent. "Why are we being hunted from
El-Kuds?"

"Because you are thought to be a Saracen
spy, and I am apostate to El Islam," he said
bitterly.

"I am not a spy," she uttered proudly.
"Who says that is a fool! And you
have not accepted Islam. You are only

'*ala sabîl Allah*,' on the way of faith in God."

"I don't care what way I'm on, as long as we're on the way out of this accursed land." He looked around nervously. If Josselyn were right, the tent should be here. His horse pricked up his ears.

"Camels!" said Kothra quietly, and broke her mount to a canter.

They found the tent pitched under a small cedar with picketed camels and sleeping servants. They swung out of the saddles, and led the smoking horses forward. A frail Syrian man came out of the tent attended by an Arab servant with a blazing cresset. O'Neill felt uncomfortable. This seemed too Arab for Josselyn's purpose. His hand went toward his sword.

"*Salâm u aleykum!*" the Syrian touched his forehead.

"*Wa aleyk es Salâm!*" Kothra answered. "And with thee be peace!"

"Have you lost your way?" the Syrian merchant asked. "Can I help?"

"I am looking for a merchant of Beyrout," O'Neill said, "to whom I was to say something and give something."

"I am a merchant of Beyrout," the Syrian answered, "dealing in silks and goldsmith's work, and amber and ambergris, and blood dromedaries. Perhaps it is I whom you seek. What is the word?"

"The word is 'Richard.'"

"And the sign?"

"This." And O'Neill handed him a sprig of broom. The Syrian merchant bowed and pointed to the tent. "If the daughter of *Iskander Thu el-Qarneyn*, of Alexander the Great, will change in the house of hair." Kothra looked at O'Neill.

"Go ahead," he told her. "It's all right." She followed the Arab servant in.

"You are now an Arabian physician of Damascus," the Syrian told O'Neill, "coming from the Hijaz with his apprentice, where you have been treating the ameers of the tribes for diseases of the eye. Your safe conduct is here signed by the Earl of Jaffa, requesting courtesy from the Seigneur of Sidon, and the Prince of Galilee. Your route is through Nablus, Samaria, Belvoir and Château Neuf. Your dress is ready when your companion is. Two racing dromedaries are prepared for you."

231

"Do you think we can make it safely?"

"It is in the hands of God," the Syrian merchant fingered his amber rosary. He had a tanned Arab face, and his hands were red with henna.

"Curse you!" O'Neill said in English. "I don't trust a damned one of you." But the Syrian was fingering his chaplet, counting the ninety-nine names of God. Kothra came out once more in Arab dress, but with none of the gold ornaments of princely houses. Also now her eyebrows were black. O'Neill went in and found Arab clothes with a black surcoat such as physicians wear. When he had dressed, he found Kothra mounted on a racing dromedary. Another was kneeling for him.

"Poor O'Neill," she said, as she saw him cross his knees on the pad, and take the single cord.

"You forget," O'Neill laughed, "that I rode these things for six months once when de Lacy lost our horses at dicing."

The Syrian merchant received their thanks with vast dignity, fingering his amber rosary with his henna tinted hands. "Good-bye,' he said quietly in English, "and good luck to both of you!" His quiet laugh answered O'Neill's "I'm damned!"

They stopped at Nablus, and slept a little at Samaria, using the Arab guest-houses, and great dignity. "*La 'allak tayib.*" "I hope thou art well?" "'*Asâk tayib!*" "And please God thou art well?" Their Arabian courtesy was overpowering. "*Allah yirda 'aleykum.*" "And the Lord be well pleased with you!" At Samaria a courier dashed through the streets with a foundering horse, and half-way toward Belvoir a patrol led by a Templar stopped them, but the passport of the Earl of Jaffa and their quiet courtesy got them through. Leaving Belvoir at night, something hissed, and Kothra said: "Look out, O'Neill, there is somewhere a serpent." But O'Neill saw the arrow half-way in an acacia tree and noted the movement in the bushes on the right. "Ride on," he told her. Through the night he heard the movement of trackers watching them on the hills and his heart sank. The sister of Ali heard them, too. But O'Neill explained it was poor lepers among the rocks. At dawn they came to Lake Tiberias, and heard the cool, grey

water lapping in the reeds. A few fisher-
boats were out, ghosting along under the
little breeze of dawn.

"I'm sorry, O'Neill," Kothra turned and
looked at him. She seemed utterly worn
out. There were lines of fatigue on her face.

"For what?" he asked.

"For that," she said, and pointed back.

And on the hills coming down toward
them, the sun shone on white habits with
red crosses on them. The sun glinted on
armour. And there was the baying of
leashed dogs. . . .

CHAPTER XI

THE morning was so gold and green, gold of sun and green of hill. The lake was gold and green. And a mile off were the fisher-boats with their brown slanted sails. The white road skirted the lake, and before them lay ruined Tiberias. The path down the hill wound like a snake, and although the riders were so near that one could hear the dogs, yet it would take them a good half hour to reach where the ripple of the lake broke on the innumerable pebbles of Galilee. Kothra brought the dromedary to his knees and slid off. O'Neill caught his saddle by the pommel and swung down.

"You see, there is no escape that way," Kothra said.

"You are right." What chance the drome-daries would have against the horses in a race was negligible, and besides, now, the country was up. There was no escape for them in fleeing. O'Neill cast a quick eye around the hill. There were the caves.

"You are forgetting the dogs, O'Neill."

He swore terribly. He raged up and down the little shore swearing. He cursed the Templars with curses more terrible than their own ritual.

"*Ya habeeby*," she said quietly, "O beloved—for now that we are both on the threshold of death, why should we conceal things? You are very dear to me, and I know, though you have said nothing, I know that I am closer to you than your own heart. Am I not?" He nodded. He could say nothing, so full were his heart and throat. "Listen, we are near death. Curse no more, O'Neill. Nor let us run any farther. Let us be proud."

He took from under his coat the heavy Meccan knife and swung it to feel the balance. "When I die," he said, " many of them will die, too. That is assured. But you, little sister of Ali, they may take you prisoner, and that I cannot bear."

"They will never take me prisoner," she told him quietly. "Look." She showed him a little dagger. "Soon I will say: There is no God but God alone; He hath no partner; His is the Kingdom; His the praise. He giveth life and death, for He is Almighty. In the name of God, the Merciful, the Compassionate. And then I shall do what must be done." He had never heard her speak so quietly, so gravely. "And for you there is a last fight, O'Neill, and God give you joy in it." She looked at him. "I don't wish to do this until the last minute. I wish to be with you until then. How much time is there?"

He watched the riders descending the hill. "Three more twists of the road, and they will come to the level and gallop. A quarter of an hour, I think."

"How lovely the morning is!" She looked around. "Never was such an autumn morning. And the little Arab fisher-boats."

"How do you know they are Arab?"

"I know them," she said, "they belong to the pasha of Edrei, on the other side of the sea. The pasha of Edrei is my father's friend."

"If you could only swim that far," O'Neill said.

"But, of course, I can swim that far," she said scornfully. "I can swim the lake. We have a summer bathing place in the pashalik of Edrei. But I cannot swim the mile in clothes."

"Then off with them, for God's sake! and save yourself."

"And leave my *rafîk*, my companion. Arabs are not like that, O'Neill."

"Then we shall go together."

She coloured crimson. "I am sorry, O'Neill. My heart is broken for it. But I cannot. You see: if you were Moslem and we were to be married, as I think we would if you were, then I would do it. But because I love you, I cannot uncover myself." Suddenly she began to cry. "If you had only said the *Fatha* in Damascus."

He was watching the riders. Another turn of the road, and they would be on the level stretch and come pounding along.

"I will say the *Fatha* now," he told her.

She came up and took his sleeve.

"I am sorry for crying, and see, I am crying no more. If you were to do that to save my life, or to marry me, I would know it later, and my heart and honour and life would be ended. Why would you say it, O'Neill?"

"I would not say it to save your life, not to have you. I say it because I accept Resignation, and I believe that in saying it I am not untrue to the Great Dervish who walked on this inland sea."

"No, you are not unfaithful to the Walker on the Lake," she looked into his eyes. "Now turn your face to the Holy Cities, and say it. And don't follow me too closely, dear one, and wait until they have thrown me a cloak from the boats."

The riders had stopped for an instant as in consultation at the beginning of the stretch. He could see the red crosses on the knights' shields, and the mastiffs pulling at the dog-boys' chains.

"*Al hamdu lillahi, Rabb el-'alamîn*, unto God be all Glory, the Lord of all worlds," he called, "the God of the Heart of Mercy, Sovereign of the Day of Doom.' He heard a splash as of a seal off a rock. "We adore Thee: we cry for help to Thee Lead us in the straight path; the path of those unto whom Thou hast been gracious, with whom Thou are not wroth, and which be not gone astray."

The riders suddenly came racing forward. Quietly, and without haste, he began taking off his physician's robes, until he stood naked and free under the golden Asian sun. He moved toward the water and stepped in. An hundred yards in front he could see the beloved head bobbing like a cork, see a white arm flick in and out of the water in a curiously child-like gesture. He took off in a long powerful drive. When he came up and shook his dripping head he heard the thunder of hoofs on the road, and an arrow plunked into the water beside him like a shallow stone flung from a sling. He dived, and swam under water until out of range, and came up laughing. Nearer came the fisher-boats, and turning over to look back he saw the chase checked by the water, and dogs standing and barking furiously, stupidly.

"Unto God be all Glory," his heart sang. He turned and swam onward. "*Rabb el-'alamîn*, the Lord of all the worlds."

THE END
OF
CRUSADE

Saint Luke Evangelist's Day
1927